little BLUE

Ana,
"Yes, Sir."
Xo, Eva Marks

EVA MARKS

Copyright © 2022 by Eva Marks

All rights reserved.

No portion of this book may be reproduced in any form without written permission from the author, except as permitted by U.S. copyright law.

This is a work of fiction. Any names, characters, places or incidents are products of the author's imagination and used in fictious manner. Any resemblance to actual people, places or events is purely coincidental or fictionalized.

Image resource: VistaCreate. This article has been designed using images from create.vista.com

A Note from the Author

Little Blue is a steamy novella, containing explicit and graphic scenes, with a few kinks thrown in the mix and is intended for mature audiences only.

About the Book

I worked for Hudson Kent for years.
He's not a man you refuse.
But I did.
Because no matter how much I wanted him, chasing the sexy, older CFO would've ruined the reputation
I worked so hard to build. It just wasn't a risk I was willing to take.
Until now.
See, Hudson isn't my boss anymore. There's nothing stopping us from acting on our mutual attraction and acting out every dirty fantasy we've ever had.
So, if he calls me now, there's only one reply I can give.

Yes, Sir.

CHAPTER ONE

Avery

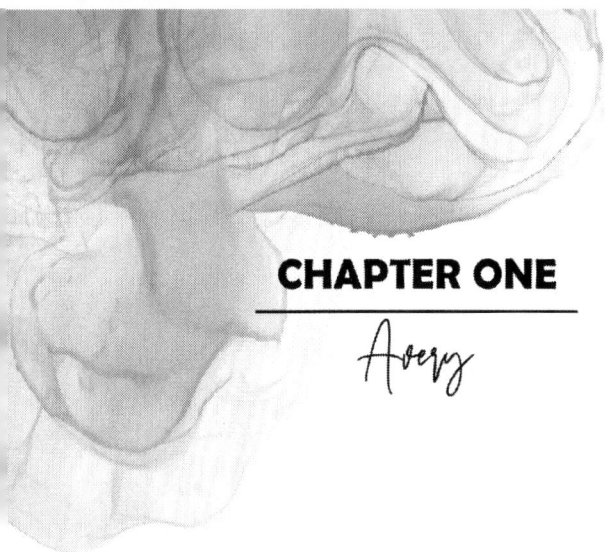

$\mathcal{P}$*ing.*

The message alert coming from my phone arrives at the end of the meeting I'm holding with my team.

It's nothing unusual. As the head of marketing at a small retail company, my cell blares at any hour of the day, from any department of our firm.

You'll never catch me complaining, though. This job at *Pearl Wilde Outfits* is a dream come true. A conscientious company, importing fashion items from organic fabrics, made in small, ethical factories around the globe, only hires friendly people, and to top it off, is a ten-minute bike ride from my apartment in San Francisco—I couldn't scream louder when they called to accept my application.

Eve Marks

It's an opportunity rarely presented to a young, twenty-four-year-old woman, even if I worked my ass off for the past three years, even if I know I can nail it. I'm grateful.

And I hustle.

That is why I don't dare glimpse at the phone while I'm talking to Anika and Cal, the members of my team. Instead, I clear my throat and place both hands on my desk. "The final topic on the agenda today is the new collection we're introducing to our online store from *Van Der Jansen.*"

Anika's brow furrows in concentration. "The line they're targeting to 16- to 25-year-olds? The one we conducted market research for last month?"

"Exactly that."

Ping.

Two texts shooting consecutively in such a short timeframe worries me. A crisis could be brewing, whether it be customer service forwarding complaints about one of our products not matching the ads, our buyers could be in the middle of negotiations and want our final opinion, or from finance, asking for help explaining the shareholders or Edna, our CEO, why this or that line stopped selling and how we're working with sales to improve it or dump it altogether.

Little Blue

But as I swipe to unlock the screen, just to evaluate whether it can wait or not, I realize it's none of these scenarios. It's not anyone from my company.

It's Hudson Kent.

The Chief Financial Officer of *Whitlock Beverages*, the company I worked for as a part of the marketing team for the past three years, the company I resigned from four months ago.

Not to mention the hottest man alive. More than hot. Impressive. Because when his six-foot-two figure with his broad shoulders and lean, narrow hips walks into a room, you can't look anywhere else. Nor can one's gaze stray anywhere else but his face, his elegantly styled short dark-blond hair, his bottle-green eyes, and smile that could kill.

Hudson Kent is a man built for seduction.

My mind knows it. My body *certainly* knows it, has known it from the day we met to the day I left *Whitlock*. Case in point, it's just his name flashing on my screen, the notification hiding the content of the messages, and already a familiar heat spreads across my body. For years his mere existence has conditioned a reflexive behavior in me, a burning that starts like a hum, low and steady in my belly, sending torturous flames up to my cheeks and down between my legs.

To say I have a crush on him would be the understatement of the millennia.

I'm yearning for him, eager to please him like I used to, and in this case—to answer him right away, whatever he might require from me.

"Don't you think we're running too fast into it?" I drop my hand quickly from its path toward the phone at Cal's question. "What about stock, shipping? Are they ready? It'll suck to put effort in and the company's money then fall short in the operations area."

"You're right, and it is moving faster than what I've been told is the norm, but *Van Der* stocked our orders as soon as Edna and the buyers gave them the green light. They're shipping it in a week, and we need to prepare accordingly. Ads, photoshoots for our website, influencers, the works."

Anika and Cal scribble notes on their notepads, their heads bowed down. I use the reprieve to snatch my phone, hesitating momentarily before hiding it under the table to conceal any content I might deem unsafe for work, which is in my case, anything personal.

At least I think it is.

Even though Hudson and I haven't spoken for the four months since I quit, I can't imagine there's a work-related topic I haven't covered with my replacement. Should he need anything professional-wise, she and the entire team are there.

So, I hope.

Little Blue

The hand holding my device quivers lightly as I unlock it, my breath catching in my throat as my thumb clicks on the messaging app.

Here we go.

Hudson: *Hey.*

Hudson: *Do you remember where we saved Brandy Crane's contract?*

Umm, what?!

His message is a slap against my logic, leaving a lot to be desired. What it doesn't do is hinder me from replying. I can't turn him down, can't tell him to ask someone else when he needs me. Once I get over the fantasy of him asking me on a date, I type my reply, adding where he can find the hard copy. I cover all bases just in case, then place the phone back on the table.

Ping.

"Cool, so we keep up the marketing for their more mature audience and add the new line separately, right?"

I nearly groan at Anika's need for clarification, though it's got nothing to do with her.

She and Cal are thorough, a lot like me, and we bounce questions and ideas between the three of us all the time. It matters little that I'm their boss, I ask and so do they whenever we need each other.

One should never reject a source of sound advice, Hudson ingrained in me throughout our numerous meetings when I'd question why he'd consult a beginner like me instead of other people in my department or my boss.

He taught me humility, another aspect of him I admired.

But I digress.

So, no, Anika's question isn't the source of my frustration. What throws me off is the inability to check for Hudson's message. His gratitude. That, unlike the first couple of messages, I'm sure I'm not mistaken about.

Hudson hasn't taken me for granted, not once, never missed a *Thank you* or *You did well* as a show of appreciation for me. I lived off this gratefulness. Did everything in my power to be blanketed with it. Was so aroused when saying my boss should be proud to have me as her employee that my nipples would pucker and my clit throbbed for him.

And four months haven't dulled out these feelings. Not even a little bit.

"Avery?"

I disturb my bottom lip, trying to contain my mounting exasperation from being withheld from what I probably missed the most about working with Hudson.

"I'm here." I offer her a smile once I've collected myself from the much-needed wake-up call. "You're right, totally separate. The last thing we want is for the client base we accumulated to get mixed signals, thinking

Little Blue

we're transitioning when we're not. Treat it as a completely separate product."

Talking to her is the wake-up call I needed, and when they write down notes, I remain focused on their faces instead of the phone. Managers, especially those who are one year older than the people on their team, don't sneak glimpses at their phones during staff meetings. They restrain their hearts from fluttering even after a consecutive ping comes.

What they do is stay present in the conversations, contribute to their discussion, and set deadlines. Eventually, the meeting has to end. When it does, they walk together back to their cubicles, out of view and it's then that I scratch the incessant itch by opening the door to a room I locked behind me months ago.

Hudson: *Little blue, I owe you one. Thank you.*

Hudson: *In fact, I'm willing to return the favor today. Dinner? On me?*

The usual giddiness I anticipated doesn't disappoint. It swathes me from head to toe, as though Hudson himself is standing here and telling me these things while using his hands to swarm over on my body as a way to emphasize just how thankful he really is.

Five long seconds are the timeline I allow myself to indulge, nothing more, before setting the phone and him aside.

I don't want to read more into it, to look for hints that aren't there.

Leaving things at that is by far the best course of action.

CHAPTER TWO

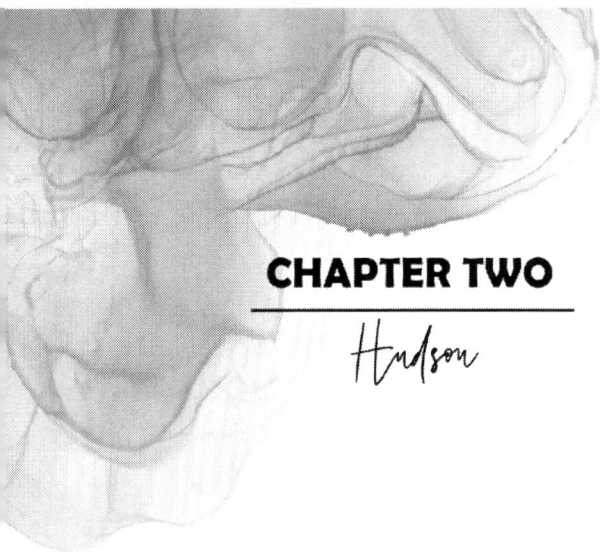
Hudson

It's late.

No employee has scurried from one end of the hall to the other in a while, and Beth, my secretary, asked for my permission to clock out for tonight some time ago. The last sun rays of the afternoon dimmed out, replaced by city lights sparkling in the murkiness of the night. Besides the silver traces of the moon and the blare from my laptop, my office is coated in darkness, where I think in peace.

While I do it often—stay behind to contemplate work-related issues free of meetings and phone calls and the like—today I haven't left my office for a whole other reason. A five-foot-three-tall woman who wears her long brown hair in a ponytail and hides her curves under business attire. Who I used to fixate on for three years when she roamed the halls of Whitlock, who I still can't stop obsessing over during the four months we've been apart.

Who avoided my last two texts even though she's read them.

Avery.

My thumb hovers above the flat screen of my phone as I wonder what to make of her non-response. I say she didn't do anything wrong, having been gracious to answer a question she must've realized people within a spitting distance could've helped me with, or suspected I remember where the damn contract is.

I couldn't have asked for more.

I shouldn't ask for more.

Yet I do.

She's always replied in one form or another to my praise of her, and I miss it. I miss her. Miss her shy smile, her eagerness to please me—professionally—on top of anyone else, her astuteness and go-getter attitude. I've missed the contrasting coyness around me and her fierce attitude for life, both sides whom I loved from the very first day I laid my eyes on her.

Ever since I saw the new girl explaining to Rina, who trained her, how outdated our research methods were, then switching from a self-assured young woman to a

Little Blue

flushed, wide-eyed girl, when I introduced myself, I was hooked.

She hasn't changed since, seeking my approval, replying as fast as lightning to my emails, calls, and texts at any hour of the day or night. I even assigned her tasks from my team, ones she could handle so we could work together.

Just to be near her, a closeness she seemed to like as much as I did.

Whenever we were together, Avery's responses ranged from reddening cheeks from the compliments I gave her, to goosebumps breaking over her delicate arms when our fingers accidentally brushed, and my absolute favorite, the subtle slide of her tongue on her bottom lip as she watched me trying to discreetly fix myself in my pants due to her presence.

I had her, in a way. Until she was gone.

So, yeah, I texted her.

And yeah, I want more from her, even though I shouldn't after being a freaking coward for three years. Her silence doesn't deter me. On the contrary, it ignites the possessiveness I didn't know I had in me and propels me into moving out of my stagnancy.

I'm done mulling over it in this office, about to act on the one conclusion I should've come to months ago.

Evan Myers

I'm going to get her, have her as mine, her body beneath me, my fingers dipping in her flesh and my cock sinking in her pussy, my soul connecting with hers. To own her.

I reach my car, kicking it into gear, reciting the name, Avery Myers to the voice command system. The ringing blares over the speakers, and I wait.

One, two.

The Tesla cruises silently through San Francisco's piers, the dark bay to my left, the tourists all gone by now.

Three, four, five.

The Golden Gate Bridge appears in the distance, its amber lights slightly covered by a light layer of fog rising from the waters. It's impressive, the sight, no matter how many times I drive past it.

Not remotely breathtaking, however, as Avery's voice as it blares in the confined space of my car.

"Hello?"

"Little blue," I say without a shrivel of hesitation, stripping away any sort of emotion from my tone besides cold confidence. "What are you doing?"

There's a pause, three seconds that I count by tapping my index finger on the wheel.

Tap, tap, tap.

"I'm home."

"Can I come over?"

Little Blue

"Hudson, it's way after midnight, and—"

"That's not what I asked, little. Can. I. Come. Over. Yes, or no?"

She doesn't say anything, but I can hear her breaths. Quick, shallow rasps that make my dick strain even harder against the zipper of my slacks.

Then the pain pulses stronger than ever when she responds by saying simply, "Yes."

CHAPTER THREE

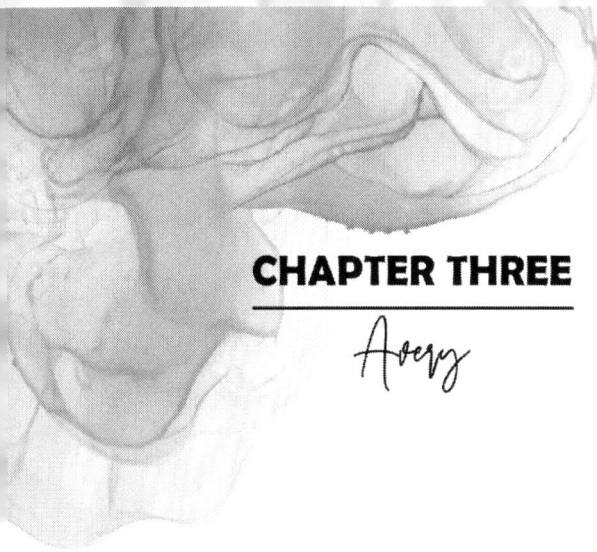

Avery

Out of all the clothes I own, why in the world did I choose this?

This is the last thought to cross my mind before buzzing Hudson into the building. I glance down at my navy chemise, realizing, as if for the first time, how thin the fabric is, how it clings to my breasts and drapes over my curves in a sea of blue satin.

It's highly inappropriate, practically see-through even with my hair cascading down the front of my body, but I don't care as much as I should. I was crazy enough to agree to have Hudson here in the middle of the night, a man my heart craves with the same intensity my body does. A man who'd undoubtedly hurt me once he leaves for good after living out our mutual fantasies on a one-night stand and leave me broken-hearted.

I think it's safe to say my clothing choice scrapes the bottom of the list of my worries.

Besides, he should be here any second, so there's no way I'm letting him wait.

I'll just have to fake confidence and hope my roommate, Jen, doesn't wake up for a pee break.

Knock, knock.

The subtle raps on the door stir me from my endless self-talk, blocking out any sort of coherent thought to the point my name feels like a distant memory.

What fills that void is acute awareness.

Hudson's here. It's really him.

Standing out there, with only one, thin, wooden door separating us.

My eyes widen; my heart walloping in my chest.

And I hurry to pull open the doorknob.

"Hey," I say. That's all I can say.

Because Hudson… Fuck. I take in the sight of him, damn near melting into a puddle on the floor. He wears a black suit combined with a smoky-gray tie, my favorite of his. It gives off a darker, more sensual air than the others, accentuating the lean muscles of the arms of a man who clearly works out but doesn't overdo it. After a short appreciation of his formal attire, my eyes trace up to his face, lingering for a beat on the five o'clock shadow that makes him look edgier than he already is, traveling up to the piercing gaze he uses to drill holes into my soul.

Whoever said *Out of sight, out of mind* was never head over heels for anyone. Not like I'm craving Hudson. My longing for him runs as deep as it did during the time we worked together, and the familiar pang of heat from seeing him sets my core ablaze.

He's intoxicating in every sense of the word. Always has been.

His lips don't break in a smile, his face a mask of dark intensity. His green eyes peruse my body leisurely, scorching my skin wherever they land, lifting back up to meet my stunned gaze. Hudson doesn't give me the slightest indication he's noticed my labored breaths or my evident arousal, despite the fact I'm still reeling from the extra few seconds he dedicated to my aching nipples.

"Hi, little blue."

For the life of me, I don't know how I move after such a masculine voice echoes in the space between us, capturing me in a chokehold and drawing me to him. But the command in his gaze, the demand I let him in, nudges me into stepping inside anyway.

Confident and assertive, he advances. Hudson possesses the aura of a man who's positive he belongs anywhere. The modest entrance to the apartment drowns

Eva Monks

in the scent of his cologne, the walls disappearing when Hudson's tall frame is all I can see.

Again, something in his demeanor speaks to me without vocalizing his wishes, a silent force guiding my feet to keep walking backward as Hudson prowls forward. My eyes are glued to Hudson, the source of the heavy electric field connecting us. The potency of it weakens my knees, and when the open kitchen appears to my left in my peripheral vision, I grasp the black counter, desperate for the support it offers.

Hudson stops about two feet away from me. Still staring, still silent.

I draw in a shaky breath. "Wine?"

"Would love some."

There's one bottle of red left, and only when I reach for it do I sever my eye contact with Hudson. I curl my fingers tightly around the neck of the bottle, aware of the trembling Hudson's presence causes my entire body. His attention remains fixed on me the entire time I work on opening the bottle, a hot, laden glare, undressing me through sheer power of will.

The more he stares, the harder it becomes to contain my shivers, resulting in me losing my hold on the corkscrew. It drops from my hand, hitting the oakwood floor in a dull thud. I fall to my knees right behind it, taking advantage of the opportunity to compose myself.

Little Blue

I bow my head, shutting my eyes, though I can't stay here long. Hudson's watching me, and if I give off the appearance of an inexperienced child, he might turn around to leave as swiftly and quietly as he entered.

Controlling my movements, I rise to my feet slowly to avoid any sudden movements that'll portray me in an even less flattering light, then halt abruptly when my eyes level with Hudson's groin. The massive breadth of his erection is barely contained in his pants, a mouthwatering sight I've encountered in the past.

At any other time, he'd have tried to conceal it.

Today, not so much.

He's still, unwavering like he wants me to get an eyeful of his desire for me. My tongue dips out to swipe over the corner of my upper lip, the hunger in me building. I'm tempted, so tempted, to discard the corkscrew, forget about the wine, and have Hudson instead.

So. Very. Tempted.

"Avery."

His stern tone is the same one he applied while talking to me on the drive over. I haven't heard him talk to me or anyone in that voice, authoritative and yet embracing, cold and hot in equal measures. It envelops me, shows me he cares, and conveys the message that if I follow his lead, life would be a clear path to the land of butterflies and sunshine.

I gulp air into my dry throat, looking up at him. "Yes?"

A shadow of a smirk pulls at his lips. It's gone before I can memorize it by heart. "Pour us the wine and let's sit. We have things to discuss."

Things to discuss.

Way past midnight, while I'm in a flimsy chemise and he's sporting a boner.

Questionable, yes, but I don't argue. I hardly ever contradict him, leaning more toward listening, learning. Admiring him. So, I follow his request, fixing us two glasses on the black, round kitchen table, occupying the chair next to the one he chose.

He slides the glass closer to him. "Thank you for this."

These four words of appreciation in these uncharted territories hit me so fiercely my heart skips a beat. It takes immense strength on my part to tame my response, to condense the immense pleasure in me into a simple nod in place of jumping him.

Hudson swirls the wine in his glass, the red liquid sloshing in slow derisive circles. "You didn't get back to me today."

Little Blue

Excuses surge out of me, even though he hasn't asked for them. "It's been a long day. I meant to, then all these meetings happened, and…"

His stoic expression tells me he isn't interested in them either. That he wanted to hear back from me and my non-responsiveness, in a way, failed him.

I shift in my seat, lowering my gaze to the stem of the glass, resigning to what I really want to say, "I'm sorry."

"Apology accepted. Next time though,"—the chair scratches the floor when he stands up—"you answer to me when I write to you, little one."

Dejection accumulates in my chest, a crippling sensation. He's about to leave. This morning I missed him, but I could've lived without seeing him again. Now it's different. Now, in the short time he's been here, having him within arm's reach, my longing for him is like another entity in the room with us, so potent I damn near scream for Hudson not to leave.

However, once more, I nod in obedience. "I will."

"I know you will."

We stare at each other as time stretches between us.

I don't beg anyone for anything, but desperation clings to me, and I think that should it make Hudson stay, I wouldn't mind doing it at all.

Yet he doesn't give me a chance to. He strips his jacket off, draping it on the back of the chair he occupied.

Ever Mine

In carefully calculated movements, Hudson unbuttons his cufflinks, rolls up the sleeves of his stark white shirt, and lowers to his knees before me.

No air comes in and out of my lungs when he rests his palms on the inside of either of my thighs, pushing them apart to reveal my ferocious desire for him.

"I know you will. Because I'm about to give you a good fucking reason to." His lungs expand, his thumbs stroking my bare skin. "Actually, make that a few."

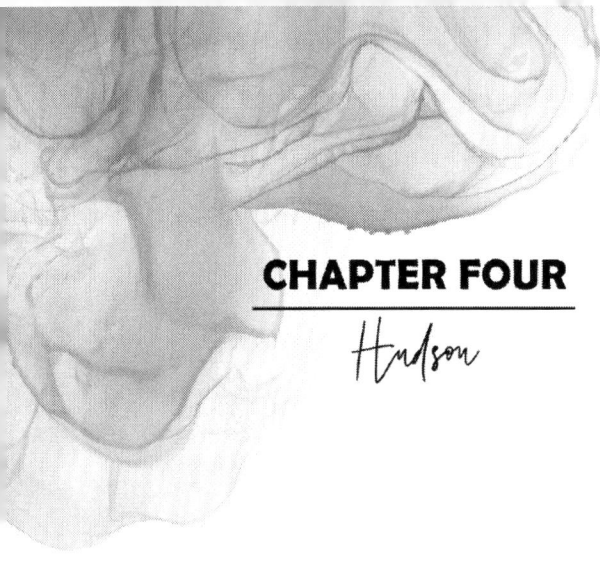

CHAPTER FOUR
Hudson

From my kneeling position on Avery's floor, the entirety of her beauty lies for my eyes to feast on. Her thighs are spread for me, allowing me the view of her satiny skin, of her blue silk lace panties. They bear the color of her nightgown, except for the darker strip dead in the middle, the soaked and ready area I'm starving for.

Any scenario I've ever conjured is surpassed by the real woman, by the feel of her flesh as it molds under my fingers. Even in my most elaborate fantasies, nothing compares to her fierce pulse beating beneath my palms, the erotic scent of her lust, or the enticing sound of her sharp intakes of air the higher I reach up her thighs.

I hold her sky-blue eyes with my green ones, exuding assertiveness, a picture of restraint, while my impatience wreaks havoc on my insides. "You ready, little one?"

She blinks twice, shifting an inch closer to the edge. To me.

"Do you want this, yes or no?" I repeat the question, my tone unwavering. It's visible she's sinking into an ocean of arousal, and I'll let her succumb to it. Soon. Now, I need her with me, I need her to say yes.

Her hips twitch at the resonance of my voice. "My roommate, Jen," she whispers, motioning with her head toward one of the closed doors. "She'll wake up."

"Then you'll just have to be very quiet." A smirk crawls up my lips, my palms skimming up to her warm center, my fingers dig deeper into the softness of her inner thighs. "Can you be a good girl for me, hold still, and be quiet?"

Avery's whimper and short bob of her head are too sweet for what I plan on doing to her, but it's obvious from the hunger in her stare that she can take whatever I bring down on her.

I continue with the stern approach, grazing the outside of her underwear, slipping my index finger under the seams. "Repeating myself will result in a punishment. Is that what you want?"

"N-no."

Little Blue

"Then speak."

Her hands clutch the seat of her chair, her knuckles whitening in her dire attempt to exhibit compliance. "Yes, yes. I won't move, I'll be quiet."

The last syllable barely leaves her mouth, and I'm already on her, sliding my fingers to part her lips. I bite the inside of my cheek forcefully, containing the growl that emanates at the feel of her slick cunt, of my thumbs sinking into her slit.

I rise higher on my knees, leaning further into Avery's body. "You're soaked. Dripping wet all over me."

Her eyes roll up her head from my unhurried strokes, her teeth nearly drawing blood to her bottom lip. She's doing her best to abide by me despite the visible progressing need to moan, to give freedom to the voracious sounds I can tell nestling in her delicate throat.

It's a heady feeling, to have this influence on her. I've never demanded anything of any woman, my ex-wife included. The urge wasn't there. With Avery though, the fixation on having her succumb to me, to follow me blindly, it consumes me. I'm desperate for it like I believe she is for me to act on those impulses.

Keeping our gazes locked, I withdraw my touch from her tight little hole, massaging her hardening clit from both sides, one thumb goes up while the other goes down. Her arousal helps them glide in either direction or to its center when I want more friction for Avery, only to end up with two fingers in her sex again.

I'm a hairbreadth from her lips, driven to taste them, and I almost do, but this game can't exist if I lose myself. A kiss from the girl who owns my dreams would undoubtedly do that, so I whisper, "You have a greedy little pussy, sucking me in like that. It makes me wonder, makes me so fucking hard thinking how it'd feel around my cock."

She looks at me, eyes half mast, barely staying afloat. Neither of us is immune to the hard blow that comes from years of unattended desire. But I'm positive she's there, got her to come to the surface to let me know as much.

As I continue to thrust my fingers in and out of her pussy, my teeth find her neck, scraping downward toward her collarbone, gliding to the swell of her breasts, hovering above one erect nipple. It gets immeasurably harder from the long, lap of my wet tongue on it, and even through the garment Avery's wearing, it tastes so fucking good. Especially when I bite her, hard.

The contact on its own doesn't break her resolve, but I start sucking on her tit while adding my thumb to flick her clit, and Avery loses the battle against her restraint.

She grips my hair, tugging at the roots, pulling me to her as she chants my name like a prayer, "Hudson, please. More, please, Hudson."

Little Blue

I remove my hands from her pussy, peeling hers from my head, and stand up. I'm towering over her, aware that my cock is directly in her eyesight.

"I asked you two things, Avery," I growl, keeping my voice low.

"I know. I'm sorry." I stop her attempts to unbuckle my belt. "Let me make it up to you."

"You don't get to decide that." Taking a step closer until my legs hit the chair she's sitting on, I push her knees apart. I'm not angry, not in the slightest. I'm hot as fuck, playing with her, and I won't be done for a long while. "Remove the nightgown from under your ass."

Avery obeys me, gazing up, her eyes bottomless pools of need.

"Hands in the air." I crouch down, raking my hands over her thighs, wrapping the hem around my fingers, and tugging it up and over her head.

She drops her arms, holding the chair like I approved of earlier.

My head shakes left and right slowly, and I tsk at her. "It's too late for that. You went against what I told you. This will be a lesson in listening. Put your hands behind you."

An indescribable surge of pleasure floods my groin, seeing her hurrying to join her wrists at her back, in the space between the metal back and the seat. I stroll to that side, pretending to be unperturbed by the whole act of submission, my cool demeanor betraying the urgency to get my hands on every part she's exposed to me.

"I'm going to tie you up, Avery. I'll never hurt you." I lower my lips to her ear. She lets out a shaky breath, her prickly skin making my dick throb painfully. "It's a lie. I will, but in a way that I believe you'll enjoy, very much so. However, if you don't, at any point, you'll say your safe word. Got one in mind or do you want me to come up with one for you?"

She twists her head slightly, a seductive grin greeting me. "Whitlock."

"You dirty little thing." I chuckle at the name of my workplace, then crouch lower to tie her wrists with her own nightgown.

Once I'm happy with how the knot's secure enough to restrict her without cutting off her blood supply, I straighten myself to take care of the second restraint, since it's not just her hands she couldn't control.

I wrap her hair around my hand, the texture is smooth in my harsh grip. She used to wear it in a high ponytail to work, those locks teasing me to capture and pull them for as long as I can remember. Her gaze is hot and begging for it, so I do, pulling harder to have her eyes up to the ceiling, to me.

Little Blue

"About those sounds you made. We need to find a solution, a way you'll remember. Open up this disobedient mouth for me."

Her lips part immediately, and I place two fingers flat on her tongue.

"Suck on them," I demand.

She does that as well, the eager little thing, her tongue swirling around me, her throat relaxes when I sink them further into her. Her apartment is dark, lit only by the low lights of the kitchen cabinets and one lamp in the living room, but I can still make out, still feel, her spit coating my fingers, how her lips curl on them pretending it's my cock.

My pulse spikes to the roof, and I force myself to stay present.

"I want you to remember this feeling." I return to bow to her ear, growling, "That fullness in your mouth, I want you to embed this exact sensation in your head when I'm eating your cunt, to remind you how to be quiet even when my name builds up in your lungs and you're desperate to scream it out. Unless it's *Whitlock*, you're to remain silent. Do you understand me?"

I remove my fingers, leaving the tip on her tongue as I wait for her reply.

"Yes."

"Good, Avery. Very good."

Eve Marks

With my heart pounding, high on administering my authority, I resume my position on the floor between her legs. My lips close around her naked nipple and I groan, sucking and licking the luscious flesh, moving to lick all the way across her chest bone, doting my attention to the other one.

After I've had my fill devouring her tits, I hook my fingers in her panties' waistband, dragging it down her body, slipping it from under each delicate foot. Her toenails are painted white, complementing her tanned skin. I kiss them, a test as well as an impulse to have my mouth on every part of her.

She spasms. That's it.

Truth is, I couldn't give a fuck less whether her roommate comes out here or not. The room Avery pointed toward is the farthest one from us, which—given the late hour and our low whispers—means there's an off chance we'll be overheard. But I can tell the quieter I ask Avery to be, the hotter her body becomes, her gaze turning more dazed and wanting with each passing second.

Besides the physical pleasure, I contribute it to Avery's anticipation for her reward, which I give her as I go up. Her foot relaxes in my palm and under the numerous soft kisses, I drape on it, continuing my path up her ankle, alternating between licking and biting up her toned calf, her tender thighs, all of her.

At an inch from her center, I grab her ass, dragging her toward the edge of her seat until her cunt is the only thing I see. It's wide open, beautiful in a soft shade of pink, and glistening with her juices.

"Not a peep out of you," I say hoarsely before I plant my mouth on her, flattening my tongue flat on her clit.

Avery shivers, the momentary loss of control resulting in her pushing her belly forward. But I can't be mad, can't bring myself to scold her as all of her, thighs, navel, pussy is in my face while I get to eat her out and connect my gaze to her piercing blue eyes.

Can't say a fucking word, except, "You taste so good."

My mouth is still on her clit, licking her relentlessly. I add three fingers to drive into her, knowing she's so close to coming she can handle it. "Sweet like everything about you."

She mouths *Thank you*, and for that, for her desperate willingness to please me, I do everything to make her feel good, to close the distance and make her come.

In the few minutes, I suck, bite, and flick my tongue on her, little Avery is fully mine. She succumbs to me, steeling herself when I circle my fingers inside her, hitting every pleasure center, stroking her G-spot over and over.

Ever Marks

"Come for me," I demand, increasing my pace both with my mouth and fingers. "Come on my mouth like the good girl you are."

As if pushing a button, like my words located the source of her innermost desires, Avery pulses around me, her ass clenching and unclenching in my palm. I don't stop, though, drawing on her orgasm while she mouths more words soundlessly until her pliant body is puddled in my hold.

I sit up to meet her eyes who are more alive than I've ever seen them, sweeping my clean hand from her jaw up to her ear, moving her hair from her reddened face. Her gaze entraps me, and I have to know what she's saying.

"Talk to me."

"Fuck me, Hudson. I want you to fuck me."

CHAPTER FIVE
Avery

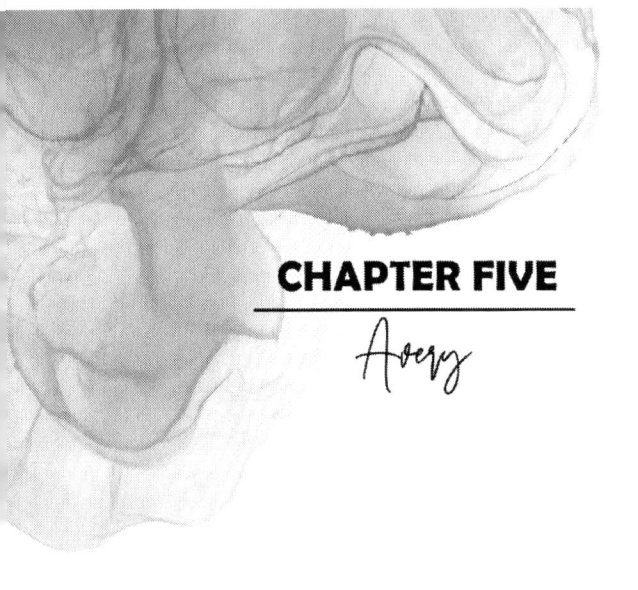

Holy. Shit.

When I gave Hudson the okay to visit me tonight, I was so confident that an explosive orgasm like the one he gave me just now would relieve the years-long tension, and get him out of my system. The itch would be scratched, the hormones and with them, the cravings would simmer down, and Hudson would become a flesh and blood man, not a god to idolize.

I'd have been sated, and in the right mind space to know this has to end soon; to tell him we had fun but it's time to go.

It made sense.

If only.

Not only am I not even halfway to the road of being satiated, but I'm also still hungry for more of Hudson.

Insatiable. Famished.

In absolute agony, and incapable of letting him go.

"What part of what we've been doing here makes you think you get to dictate anything?" he asks from behind me.

The intoxicating sensation of his fingers as he undoes the knot he secured my wrists with renders me silent, the feeling of the fabric caressing my skin on its path as it releases and drops to the floor nearly causes my heart to stop.

I don't speak, accepting quietly Hudson's large palms on my skin.

He massages the raw areas I scratched harder from my battles with myself to remain in place when the force of the climax hit me, a potent yet tender touch.

Coming to stand in front of me, he speaks in a low voice meant for my ears alone, "I choose how to pleasure you, I choose what to do with you. Understood?"

His harshness isn't intended to intimidate me. It's all part of the hottest play I've ever experienced in my short sexual history. And apparently, it affects Hudson the same way. He's facing me anew, his cock hard, pressing against his pants. I'm tempted to cup it, stroke on it, suck on it, and swallow his cum. Been tempted to do it for so long, and now that it's appropriate, now that he's inches away, I…

I don't.

Hudson taught me tonight that obeying him over my most basic impulses is an erotic pleasure in its own right. So, since he didn't say I can speak, I simply nod.

"Very good, little one." He pairs my thrill of submission with his praise, tilting my head higher by grabbing my chin. "However…"

His tongue does this sensual skim across his upper lip, brief torture leading to a release coming from his words. "There's no way in hell I'm leaving without being inside you. Get up."

My legs haven't straightened before he scoops me in his arms. My heels cling to his waist, my body supported by his hands under my butt and I'm being carried to my room. The night lamp casts an amber glow in the intimate space, a soft touch added to the feminine white and cream-colored decor.

I glance from my queen size bed to him, thinking that's where he'll throw me next.

His sinful smirk is immediate as he shuts the door swiftly. He's so strong, turning us to the side and stilling himself like I weigh nothing. We're close and I long to kiss him, taste myself on his lips, feel his short stubble scraping my chin.

But not without his okay, which he withholds from me, twisting his head toward the full-length door mirror. "Look at yourself."

True to my resolve, I turn to where his eyes are cast.

An exhilarating yet terrifying notion flashes behind my eyes.

We make a gorgeous couple.

Hudson releases the hand that's closer to the mirror from behind, twisting his long fingers around my hair, pulling on it, and saving me from dwelling on wishes I have no business entertaining.

Instead, I concentrate on Hudson's hand, his grip, on the desire it builds in me, on what I see in the mirror, beyond my wishful thinking. I will myself to see Avery and Hudson, the people who worked together, who are playing a dangerous, sexy as fuck game.

That's all there is to it.

Until he goes and melts my heart. "You're beautiful, you know that?"

"M-hmm," I manage.

"You're allowed to talk." His lips come to my neck, teeth nibbling along the length of it. "And I want to hear you say it, say you know you're beautiful because you're about to spend a long time looking and loving this precious face when I fuck you from behind. You're going to witness every single feature on your face contort with hurt, then morph into pleasure. Maybe both. And you'll love it."

Hudson tugs on my hair harsher when my talking diminishes into a moan. "Say yes, blue."

"Yes, Sir."

At that, Hudson ceases the delicious sucking of my throat, relieving some of the pressure from my hair. His slight shock is parallel to mine, but I don't care. I refuse to take it back. Tonight is about pure unadulterated *feelings* and if this is how he's making me feel, so be it.

There's no comment from his end either, only commands as he lowers me to the floor, "Face the door, hands up." Then he leaves me to go lean against the door.

I stay put, lifting my hands high, bare under his watchful, dripping-with-sensuality gaze, the anticipation sizzling between my legs.

"Come here," he beckons me to him, his finger mimicking the curling it did inside my cunt, and it's a wonder I'm capable of any move whatsoever.

The floor is warm under my bare feet that deliver me to him until he raises his palm to signal me to stop. He lowers his chin in acknowledgment, then proceeds to shove himself from the wall and strip off his shirt, button by button.

His mouthwatering, broad, flat chest is revealed once he shrugs it off, a light smattering of blond hair covers his taut belly just above, and probably below, his belt.

The intense stare he's been giving me shifts to where my hands hang in the air. It doesn't escape me that he hasn't discarded his shirt, and as he reaches for my wrists, I get a strong sense of why.

Hudson's ironed shirt crumples when he uses it as his other choice of a rope for my wrists. He loops the sleeve to secure my wrists again, dragging me to the door hanger where he fastens the other sleeve on the door hanger above my mirror.

I study our images in the mirror, his wider and taller figure moving to loom behind me, his hands mold into my waist, down to my hips. I succumb to him fully, leaning back to let him have me any way he likes, trusting him with my body. A shuddering moan nearly bellows from me when Hudson places his palm flat on the curve of my spine.

"I told you to stop holding back." He views me from the mirror, and I do, letting out a pained sigh, though the both of us are aware it's the attention he dotes on me that's the embodiment of pleasure.

Our gazes meet, the darkness and want in his eyes visible, though he handles me with patience, a mesmerizing equanimity in his touch. He slides his palm

Little Blue

down leisurely, applying pressure at the crack of my butt, opening me up, resuming his journey up, repeating it again and again.

His other hand grips my hips, rocking me to him, building the pressure in my stomach I can hardly contain anymore. Then, without any preamble, his palm leaves my back to strike one of my ass cheeks. The sound of the clap echoes in my room, but Hudson stands there as though nothing has happened.

The surprise forces a yelp out of me. The pleasure that ensues leaves me yearning for more.

Hudson's head tilts, one of his eyebrows cocks up. "Do you have anything you want to say?"

He's asking for my safe word. I shake my head, angling my butt an inch higher. "No, Sir."

"Avery. This is a tiny part of what I fantasized about doing for three years. Worse things than this even." A second smack lands on my ass, creating another burst of heat that scorches me, damn near making me come again.

Hudson's palm is in the air for the third time, and I clench my teeth in preparation, refusing to give in to my cravings unless I'm full with him.

"Each one of these fantasies, I'm giving them to you, blue," he says on the last spank.

When he leaves me, it's to unbutton his pants and extract a condom from one of his pant pockets. He pushes down his pants and boxers with his free hand, pressing the thick cock I've only ever got a glimpse of through his pants to my behind. He feels bigger than I imagined, and I shudder with absolute pleasure.

"And you're going to take it all like the good girl you are."

CHAPTER SIX
Hudson

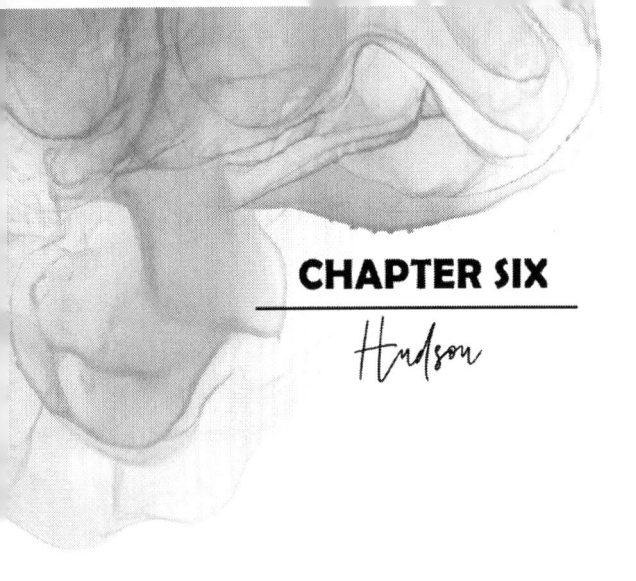

"Yes, Sir."

She repeats the use of the title, the word I didn't realize I needed to hear this badly. The thrill from it sends wild currents from her pouty little mouth straight to my ears, my heart, my throbbing cock.

This powerful woman who made a name for herself in our firm by the age of twenty-two, who landed a managerial role by twenty-four, *she* bends to *my* will. In this bedroom, she trusts me to reign over her, resigning the control of her body to me.

There's no reason for Avery to believe I won't dish more than she can take, but she does. She trusted me as I spanked her soft, hadn't breathed a singular vowel from the harsher ones I administered that left pink marks on her delicate flesh.

She gives herself to me, a gift I'll show her I'll treasure, prove to her that her trust isn't misplaced. Even after three years of abstaining from sex, reluctant to be with anyone who isn't her, I can and will control both her and myself.

"Perfect. Docile and willing to please me. That's how I like you, blue. How I've always liked you." The admission flows from me naturally, claiming what I've always wanted, what I want for a lifetime.

It doesn't rattle her either, judging by the lust etched on her face—the parted lips, misty eyes, a sheen layer of sweat covering her smooth forehead—she's in it with me. And my pretty little girl is going to get fucked so hard she would've been heard from a soundproof basement.

Just after I get her wet, beautiful cunt spread all over me. I place the condom on her back, guiding my dick to her pussy, groaning when she clamps her thighs on me once the head of my cock slides on her clit.

I hold it, drawing circles around her clit while holding her gaze through the mirror. "So fucking desperate for me to fuck you."

"I am,"—her voice is choked, tits bouncing when I push her, my stomach slapping against her ass—"Sir."

My balls tighten with each stroke, and it's all that I can do not to come on her. I draw back, gripping the condom and dragging it across her sensitive skin across her butt, giving her another form of friction, of heightening her already fired up senses.

The pleased sounds emanating from Avery push me to roll the condom on faster, to be wrapped and ready for her. After I do, I position myself at her entrance, driving the tip of my cock inside her warm sex. I play with it, play with her, thrusting a little more of me each time. I grip the front of her waist in the curve connecting her crotch and her tender lower belly, pulling her to me.

Her cunt pulses around me, enveloping me, begging me to drive my entire length into her.

"Hudson." My name echoes just as sweet from her lips as *Sir* did. Reverent, needing me to take her.

And she's been so good, it's time. Her hair wounds perfectly in my palm, her head angling higher, exposing her slender neck in the mirror. I marvel at the image of her, tied in my shirt, her chest exposed, her breasts heavy with lust, nipples erect. And of everything laid out in front of me, my favorite part is her face, the innocent girl she is, and the savage woman who begs me to be rough.

I draw out of her slowly, then shove all the way in the same instance, yank her hair harder as I do. I study her reflection, restraining myself when I notice the dampness in her eyes.

"You have your safe word."

She glares at me intently, saying nothing.

"But you don't want to use it." I rear back, repeating the shove and tug whenever I thrust. "You. Like. Being. My. Little. Slut."

We're hyperventilating, sweating, and our shared lust is explosive as it spreads between us. I release her long, silky locks, curling my fingers around the front of her neck. "My beautiful slut, you take my cock so well."

Avery's panting, pushing against me, urging me to test her further. I glide my hand up her jaw, tilting her head up so her ear is in my mouth.

"Eyes on the mirror."

Her blue irises lower to look at me.

"Want me to go harder?"

"Yes."

"Make you come so fucking hard you'll be sore for days after?"

"Oh, God, yes."

I slide my hands to stroke her down there, going slow even though I can feel her walls clenching, her nub swollen beneath my middle finger. "Beg for it, little blue." With a flick of my finger on her clit, she shivers in my arms. "Beg for me."

"Christ, yes, Hudson, fuck me."

"You can do better than that." My index finger joins the middle one, both moving faster.

"Hudson." Her grip tightens on the sleeve of my shirt, her back arches. "Please, I'm begging, I need you. Fuck me, make me come. I'll do anything, just make me come."

"Good girl." I thrust into her deep in one push, up to the hilt. My teeth sink into her bare shoulder, tasting the salt on her skin. "I knew you could do it."

"Thank you. Thank you," she pants, melting into me.

My hips roll, each stroke hitting her faster and harder. I'm not letting her move forward though, holding her tight so she'd feel every inch of me. Her warmth morphs into scorching heat, so hot it makes it virtually impossible to hold back.

"Now. Come on me this fucking second."

"Fuck, Hudson," she manages to say before she shudders in my arms, her knees buckling and her entire body weight drops into me. Her pussy clenches as the force of her climax swipes over her, and I'm right there with her.

A profound release thrashes my body, white light behind my eyes from coming the hardest I ever have. Avery, the only thing I can grasp under the power of my orgasm, becomes everything to me. I stroke her hair, my stare softening when I tell her, "I'm so pleased with you."

Her head swivels to me, and a lazy, satisfied smile creeps up on her face. "Thank you."

Those lips. I'm done waiting to kiss them. I lean over, pressing my mouth to hers, moaning when her tongue slides out to meet mine.

"The restraints," I murmur, not wanting to separate from her yet needing to. She's been held up long enough. Making a quick move of sliding out and discarding the condom in the trashcan by the door, I walk over to hold her front.

"I'm removing the shirt, but one hand will still support you, okay?" I tuck away strands of hair that stuck to the sweat on her face, my harsh side replaced by the gentleness she deserves. I guide her head to relax and be supported by my chest, proceeding to untie her wrists. "I got you."

"Okay."

The tight bonding along with the tugging and pulling from the night left red marks on Avery's skin, and even though she doesn't complain, doesn't shake them for relief, I'm sure she's in some form of pain. I kiss the inside of the left, then the right, doting my attention on either before moving her hands to round my neck.

"There you are," I smile when her arms drape over my shoulders, her forehead fitting into the crook of my neck.

She's feeble, unable to do anything except put her weight on me. Carefully, I bend low to scoop her up, carrying her to her bed where she can rest more comfortably. I cocoon her further by enveloping us in her crema-colored covers, covering her naked body, making her feel treasured.

Her big blue eyes study while I tuck her in, remaining still until I'm done. She says nothing when I cup her reddened cheeks, her dark eyelashes fluttering just barely when she sees me descend to her mouth.

As I did while I held her, I brush my lips on hers, light as a feather. My insides explode at resuming the intimate connection, my heart soars from the gentle touch of her palm over mine, of her eagerness to deepen our kiss. She tastes so sweet, but I have to pull away.

Lowering my chin, I raise my brow, caressing her cheek with my thumb. "You okay?"

"Yeah." The loss of our connection apparently impacted her somehow, because her drowsy expression sobers up. Her next kiss on my cheek is quick, a second later I see her wiggling off my lap and hugging her knees to her chest. "I'm great. Better than great."

I'm lost as to what I did to have her act defensively, though I keep it to myself. I can't grasp exactly what we did myself, so, I can't expect her to. We both need time to talk. Until then, I can offer her my comfort. "Would you like me to spend the night?"

"No." Her small palm reaches from under the covers to rest on my shoulder. She smiles, the fond, Avery smile I remember. "Thank you for asking. I'm so happy you came, um, literally too,"—her chuckle relieves some of my concerns—"but I think I'm just going to crash. Alone."

Trying to not take it personally, I study her face for any clues she might be in pain. "You sure you're fine?"

"Definitely. Don't worry about it, Hudson."

I pull her to me into another kiss, conveying through my actions that I'm here for her. All she has to do is say the word.

"Time to go," she mumbles against my lips.

"All right."

We get up, and I retrieve my clothes while she slips into a silk blue robe. She truly seems to be doing okay, even in the silence following us on our short walk to her doorstep.

"Good night, little." I lean forward, kissing her forehead.

"Night, Hudson," she says, then adds when I'm almost out of earshot, "I'll never forget you."

As I ride down the elevator, I promise myself she won't ever have to.

CHAPTER SEVEN
Avery

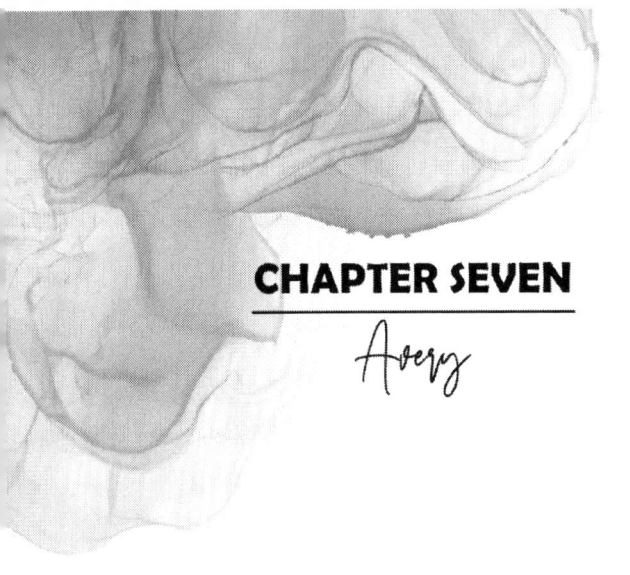

The alarm on my phone goes off at six-thirty.

I roll my eyes, groaning as I search for the source of the offending noise on my nightstand. The room is fairly dark other than the light on the screen, making the phone easy to find. I shut off the alarm, throw my feet off the bed, and shuffle out to the bathroom.

Through the entire process, I keep my eyes half-closed, gripping hard onto last night, refusing to welcome the new day. Hudson isn't here anymore, and the sun filtering in is all the reminder I need that I'm on my own, without him, but my brain begs to stay in yesterday. Just for a little.

Ever Marks

Instead of brushing my teeth like I intended to, I bring a strand of my hair to my nose, inhaling his potent masculine scent that belongs to him and him alone. Another man could wear his cologne, bathe in his soap, yet they'd never smell like him.

"We'll always have Paris," I mumble the famous quote from the movie *Casablanca*, letting my hair fall to the side.

And then I notice it. "My wrist." I lift the other one that bears identical, light red marks. They're mild, barely there, yet their presence sends a pang of longing to my heart. I can't stop admiring them throughout the shower, when I look in the mirror as I dry my hair, and while pacing through the kitchen toward my room wrapped up in a towel.

Which is probably how I miss Jen standing there. "Morning sunshine, what are you looking at there?"

Her gaze shifts to where my eyes have been. It takes her less than a second to put her steaming coffee mug on the counter, scurry to where I stand, and grip both my wrists.

"What the…?" She twists them so my palms face up, twists them in the other direction, and runs her thumbs on the light burn marks. "What is this? Is this from last night?"

Little Blue

Heat rises to my cheeks, and it's becoming obvious I can't lie to her. Besides, I've got nothing to hide. Hudson didn't do anything I didn't want him to.

"There's this guy…" I start, raising my eyebrows emphatically. "A good guy."

"A good guy," she repeats, studying me through her large brown eyes. "This wasn't forced?"

"Good guy yes, forced nope." A smile curves my lips up, the memory of Hudson surrounding me. His sweet caresses, of the consideration he applied after fucking me senseless. He's more than a good guy, he's the perfect guy.

"Okay, a good guy who likes it rough. Sweet." Soothed by my affirmation, Jen winks at me, releasing my hands to return to where she was perched on the kitchen counter. Since her mornings start later than mine, she's still in her pajamas, her black hair pinned in a messy bun on top of her head. "I would've died if he did something to you while I put music on to mute the two of you."

"Nothing like that." My teeth show as my grin widens. "Whatever he did, I wanted it. Really, really, really wanted it."

"The guy gets three reallys, huh? Is it serious?" She wags her eyebrows. "No one you've dated landed three of these or those starry eyes for that matter."

"He's something else, for sure."

"Sooo…when am I meeting him?" She practically hops up and down now, adding excitedly, "On a double date, maybe? You, me, Briar, and Mr. Else?"

My grin falters. Despite Hudson's kind offer to stay with me, I'm not under any illusions that he's looking for a serious relationship with a girl my age.

"I can wait. I remember what a beginning of a relationship's like. Take your time, bleed him dry, sis."

Her choice of words causes a chuckle to burst from my lips. "No, it's not that. I won't be seeing him anymore."

"Triple-Really man? No?" I don't mind the nickname she gave to him, he might as well have earned it. "What's wrong with him?"

"Nothing, aside from, well…" I stumble on my words, second-guessing how to say what is a sore memory for my friend. "Join me while I dress? I want to make it to work on time without speed-pedaling."

"Right behind you."

Each of our rooms has a large, white-wood closet decorating almost an entire wall. I slide one door open, grabbing black panties and a nude bra to go with the outfit I planned for today of black slacks and a cream blouse.

"Remember Richard?" I pull up my underwear, then give Jen my back to hook on my bra.

Little Blue

Jen snorts, loudly. "Of course, the unforgettable Dick."

"So, this *guy*"—I avoid saying his name because he won't return and it doesn't matter—"he's sort of a Richard."

I go to retrieve my outfit in time to catch Jen twisting her lips in disgust. "An older man who uses younger women as placeholders until someone more mature who wants a family comes along? Fucks whoever's dumb enough to fall for his act? Who can't bother responding to texts?"

"He's okay where texting is concerned." Hudson, by asking to stay and take care of me, proved to be more compassionate than I gave the smoldering man credit for. And while he might not play me on purpose, I don't see him wanting to settle down with someone thirteen years younger than he is.

"For now."

A defensive response forms on my tongue, given that Hudson hasn't once ignored my texts or calls, one I eventually shove down my throat. No point in arguing over a man I'm not and wouldn't date. Even if he deserves it.

"I guess, yes." I dress quickly, moving to observe myself in the door mirror. Hudson's shade lingers behind me, reminding me of the way he held me yesterday and the overwhelming feel of him renders me silent for a beat.

"All I'm saying is be careful." Jen comes to hug me from behind, resting her chin on my shoulder. "Have fun, but don't overlook the red flags, you know?"

My shoulders sag, my lips twisting. "Yeah, I know."

"Change of subject! Sorta," she exclaims, hopping to my side. "Old guy can really hit it, can't he?"

"Yes, he can. He really, really, really can," I say, with a stern face before we both crack up.

She rubs my arm affectionately, grinning at our reflection. "Then don't let me or my past ruin it for you. As long as you're careful with your heart, fuck his brains out. The minute he starts acting shady, kiss his sorry ass goodbye."

I let what Jen said sink in while I'm pulling open one of my shoe drawers, when the buzzer of the intercom rings, startling us.

"Are you expecting—" we start simultaneously, each of us referring to the other's guy.

"Briar isn't supposed to be here until tonight," she answers, heading for the door and out of my room. "Stay here, finish your arrangements, I'll check on why in the world someone would think it's acceptable to be here before eight in the morning."

"Thanks," I call out.

Little Blue

I slip on my flats, grab my bag, take one more look at my reflection then follow Jen to the door since I need to get my butt off to work anyway. I'm out of my room, lowering my brow in confusion.

"Who was that?" I ask Jen who's holding the door open, sneaking glances into the hall.

"Flower delivery." She half-turns to me, her eyes glinting. "For you."

"For me?"

"Yup. Not bad, Mr. Triple-R."

The delivery guy appears in the doorway, a bouquet of stunning blue carnations in his hand. "Avery Myers?"

"That'd be her." Jen's enthusiasm manifests in her voice.

"Yeah." My mind has a hard time wrapping around the huge bouquet presented to me, and by the time my focus returns and I put the bouquet on the floor to tip the guy, he's gone.

The vase with which the flowers arrived in has a silk red ribbon tied around it. A small envelope is tucked between the ribbon and the glass. I crouch on the floor, pulling it out.

"It's really, really, really him, isn't it?" Jen closes the door, staring at me from above.

I can't help laughing at her nonsense, although my heart is pounding so hard, I can hardly speak. "Yeah."

"Want to read it alone?"

This is why she's my best friend. She gets me. "Yeah, thank you."

"Don't mention it." She sends another one of her big smiles at me, waltzing back inside the apartment.

In the privacy of the empty corner of the house, I open Hudson's letter.

Blue,

I can already imagine you wrapped in this ribbon like a gift for me.

Save it for the next time we meet.

Yours,

Hudson

Butterflies flutter in my stomach, my cheeks heat up, and I damn near forget how to breathe. The giddy sensation envelops me, driving me to listen to Jen's encouragement of having fun for the sake of it, to be clever, and to know when to hop off.

Problem is, the time to jump ship was yesterday. I've already developed feelings for him, emotions that intensified after the intimate caresses I'll have trouble forgetting for the next millennia. Fun with Hudson can't be simplistic, and I'm hurting as it is from the mere idea of saying goodbye. I can't be the person Jen wants me to be.

And so, not without effort, I get up, leave the apartment, texting Hudson on my way down the elevator

Little Blue

the only response that'll spare me a bigger heartache than the one I'm nurturing, and though it pains me to write it, to not have more of him, I type out, *Thank you for the beautiful flowers. I love them, but I can't do it another time. I hope you understand. I'm so sorry.*

I'm confused, conflicted, wondering if it's the right course of action.

Hudson, however, feels nothing of the above.

I know this because he's calling me.

CHAPTER EIGHT
Hudson

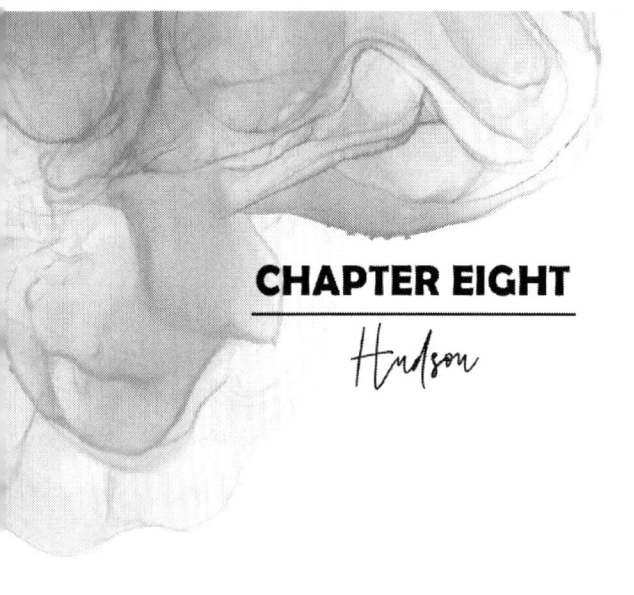

I hurt Avery. If she doesn't want to see me again, I must've done something she hasn't complained about. And this beautiful girl is hurting now because of me.

Knowing the two of us were high on sex, releasing years' worth of pent-up energies into one hour does little to assuage my guilt. I was in charge of her, and I failed.

I'm at the office when the text from her pings on my phone, going through emails, clearing out the desk before the company's big public signing of Brandy Crane. The PR for Whitlock Beverages arranged for the press to be here from nine to noon, speeches to be held by the heads of our company and Brandy. In short, a media circus.

Eve Marks

It's a big deal, even for a major player like us, but at the moment I don't give a flying fuck about any of it. I dial Avery's number, her wellbeing overrides whatever it is I have going in my life.

"Hello?"

"Avery." I summon all the stillness in me to soothe whatever turmoil I caused her yesterday. "How are you?"

"I'm good. Climbing my bike and off to work." There's shuffling in the background. "You're on my AirPods, so it might get windy. Sorry about that."

"Don't be, I hear you just fine."

And what I hear alleviates my concerns almost entirely. She sounds friendly. Free of the barriers of the workplace and void of regret brought on by last night, her sweet voice carries over to me from the other line. I exhale, a long, silent breath of relief, relaxing in my chair and looking up at the ceiling.

Thank fucking fuck.

"Hudson? You wanted something?"

Her breath quickens as the seconds tick by and I don't respond, a stark reminder of the sweet, short rasps for air when I was buried balls-deep inside of her. Pressure builds in my groin, along with my confidence. "I'm here. Did you like my flowers?"

I deliberately avoid asking why she said no. Unless it's regret, I have no plans on giving up on Avery.

Little Blue

"I did, and they're beautiful, but listen…"

"They can't be as beautiful as your eyes." I close mine, picturing her on her bike. I'd sometimes see her, on the rare occasion we made it to the office at the same time, the adorable, young woman, with her ponytail bouncing, her red cheeks from the ride. Every day that started like that was almost always a good one. A great one. "But then again, I don't imagine too many things can compare to your beauty."

"Thank you." She's back to talking in that grateful voice. It means I still have that effect on her.

If I had any doubts we were a one-time thing, they're eliminated now. I'll give her all of me, a man at her disposal a man who'll be strict while cherishing her, who'll be attuned to her every need.

I'm willing to open my heart to her, at last.

"You're welcome." I tap a pen on the top of my desk, watching the sun rising higher in the sky. "I want to see you tonight."

There's a pause in the low thrusting of the wind, a red light she's stopped at, I'm guessing. "We can't do this."

On the off chance that I'm wrong, I ask one more time, "Did I hurt you?"

The wind picks up again when she says, "I would've said…the word."

"Emotionally, Avery." Because her heart, that's what I care about. "Are you okay with what we did?"

"I am. Gosh, it's weird discussing it like this."

"Little one." Resting my pen down, my thumb grazes my bottom lip, my mind wandering to all the ways I can pleasure her. "I want to touch you, be with you. Don't you want to please me?"

"Yes." Her agreement is more of a huff of air.

I bring the speaker close to my lips, lowering my voice to a mere whisper, "Are you wet?"

"Y-yes."

"Mmm. Then you'll be ready for me when I plunge two, then three fingers in your soaked pussy while I eat you out. I want your legs to shudder on my shoulders when you come." My hand clenches into a fist, and I shift in my seat when my cock pushes at my gray suit pants. "And you'll lie in my arms after, get spoiled while I tell you what a good girl you are."

The line is silent. "Okay."

"Okay, what?" A smirk tugs at my lips, the thought of spending the evening with her more appealing than any endorser ever could. "You need to say it."

"Yes, I want to come." Her groan is followed by a short laugh. "I want *you* to come over. I want to see you."

A knock on the door draws me from the woman who has my heart on a leash. I avert my gaze from the

Little Blue

windows to the door, where Andrew Jameson, the CEO of Whitlock stands. He walks in, his charcoal-gray suit is a brand new one for the occasion, I assume. Whenever he enters like this, without a meeting or waiting for an invite, it means my full attention is required, especially on a day like today.

"I need to hang up, I'm starting a meeting. Have a good one." I give Andrew my usual smile, grateful for the desk separating us.

"You, too." She hangs up, and the line goes dead.

I raise my head to meet Andrew, listening to him run down the schedule for today, feigning excitement I don't share with him, not today.

Not while I twist my pale-blue tie between my fingers, contriving one fantasy on top of the other, of how I'll put it to use, in less than a few hours.

Let the countdown begin.

CHAPTER NINE
Avery

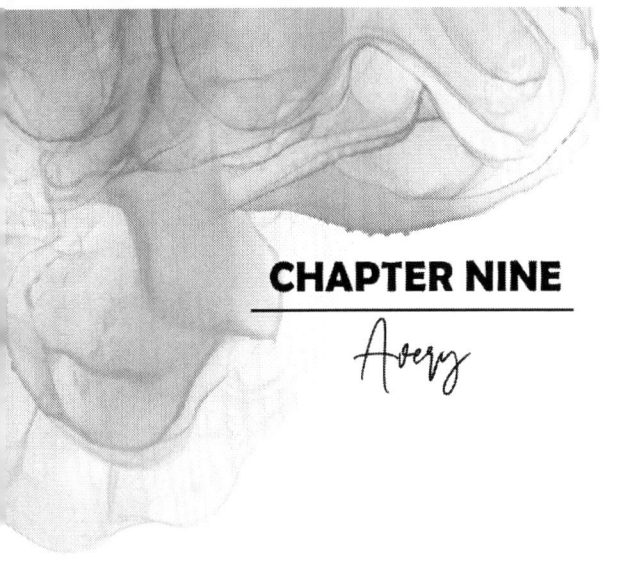

"What are you wearing?" Hudson's commanding voice casts a warm glow over every part of me.

Ever since he called me this morning, I've been on the edge, fighting to concentrate at work, squirming in my chair whenever visions of what he might do to me permeated my mind.

I crave him, despite knowing I'll be left hanging, ruined when we reach the inevitable end. His looks, his touch, his attention, they weave the net Hudson casts to capture me, and I'm powerless to swim in the direction of safety. If he would've just let go after yesterday, I would've remembered that night for a long time, eventually writing it off as great sex. I'd have let it go, someday.

But I can't say no to him. His insistence earlier, coupled with the flowers and care, they're too much for me to fend off. My stomach churned through meetings, lunch, and on my way home. My body is worn out from last night, and still, I waited until this late hour for his call.

And hearing his voice, it's all worth it.

"My blue chemise from yesterday." I hesitate, rushing to explain, "I washed it."

"You're fucking adorable." His masculine, low rumble of a chuckle sends a shiver straight down to my core. "We can't have you going out to the street like that, now can we?"

"To the street?" Curiosity captivates me. "At this time of night? Are we going out?"

"So. Fucking. Adorable." The humor is gone from his tone when he draws out a long breath. "You still have that black button-down shirt and black tight skirt?"

Having him specify two garments I have in my closet should've surprised me.

It did the opposite.

"Yes." I'm thrilled, rushing to my closet, shrugging off my nightgown mid-walk.

"I'm happy."

I stop where I stand, taking a second to compose myself. I wonder if he has the slightest clue what it does to me, how it affects every cell, how it makes me wet instantly.

"Put them on for me."

The clothes are out, thrown on my bed. "Anything else?"

"Your ballet shoes." I'm about to ask which, the high of being controlled to the very last detail intoxicating me. He beats me to it, though, assuming his place in our dynamic as the leader. "The black ones. Fix your hair in a ponytail as you did for the office, and bring the ribbon down with you."

"Yes, Sir," I breathe out, my heart too big for me to speak.

He lets out a groan of approval. "Dress up and meet me downstairs. You better not make me wait, little one."

Before the call even ends, I'm grabbing my skirt, pulling it on. My wetness spreads across my inner thighs from the wriggling movements, the touch of the fabric on my sensitive clit feels like feathers on my frayed nerves. And that's without even laying eyes on Hudson.

As fast as I can, I button up my shirt, leaving the two top buttons undone, then shove the hem inside my skirt. It's a tight fit, which I assume Hudson remembered, too. While I slide my shoes on, I can't help but feel my arousal rising, and I fumble out of the room.

Ever Marks

I'm no longer tired or fearing heartbreak. I'm full of life, anxious to be held by him. Because even if it scares me, I can't deny it anymore. His voice alone throws me in a cage I'll happily stay locked in for however he demands, and I'll happily indulge in it however long we might have together.

The elevators take forever to reach me, longer to get to the ground floor. I haven't considered how slow they are until today when I'm so desperate to see him, I almost yank them open myself when the car stops.

Breathless, I scour the dimly lit lobby like a starved person would upon smelling the slightest hint of food. He's not here, but my phone ringing tells me he's not far away.

"Did I make it in time?"

"You're perfect." The sound of him, confident and so in-charge, washes over me. "You trust me, don't you?"

The truth behind what I'm feeling is complicated. With my safety? Sure. With my heart? Very debatable. My response isn't helpful to either of us. It'll ruin the moment, which I'd rather avoid. "Yes."

"You should. Come outside," he demands. "Once you're there, hang up, close your eyes, hands clasped behind your back with the ribbon in your palms. Wait for me there."

Little Blue

"Yes." I tread out of the building, my hand hovering above the handle. "Sir."

The line goes dead. I brace myself, the cool summer breeze welcoming me into the night while the slight dread of being alone out here filters into my consciousness. Jen and I live in a safe neighborhood, though you wouldn't catch me riding the bike or jogging on my own any later than nine in the evening.

Trust Hudson, I tell myself, releasing the fear, committing to him. My clit throbs from the simple shift in awareness, from being secure no harm will come to me.

He promised. I believe him.

And he's here. There's a presence at my back, a net of electricity. I know Hudson's there without him having to utter a word.

"I wish you could see yourself," he whispers against my neck, causing my already high-strung nerves to wind tighter. He traces a finger down from my shoulder to where my wrists meet, grabbing them with one hand while the other one circles the side of my throat. "So fucking beautiful. So mine."

I don't breathe a sound, too immersed in this fantasy he's playing out to believe anything other than what comes out of Hudson's mouth. This evening he's my Sir, and I'm his. It's the beginning and the end of it.

Eve Myers

I release the grip on the piece of silk clutched in my fingers the second he tugs on it. He lowers the hand that's on my throat to my wrists, a thumb from each of his palms caressing the mildly sore skin, and I lean into his healing touch.

"Think you can be tied again?"

"Yeah," I respond honestly.

I've been itching for his hands the whole day, daydreaming of floating on the transcendence I get from his strong touch restraining me like he does now. The pleasure is immense, the anticipation for Hudson's next move only adds to it.

The scent of his cologne sharpens as he places a soft fabric over my eyes, tying it, at the back of my head below my ponytail.

"My little blue wearing my tie," he muses, his voice emanating in the space in front of me.

He's quiet for a while after that, letting the tension simmer with each passing moment. My breasts swell at the notion of his deep, green gaze on me, from the notion of his eyes drifting across my body in my tied and blindfolded state.

"Perfect," he announces in a steely tone, spiking the temperature of my blood well into the hundreds. I'm captivated by it, which is why when Hudson grips my bicep lightly and simultaneously rests a hand on the top of my head I flinch.

"Shh. It's me. Let's get you in the car." He directs me into the passenger seat, fastens my seatbelt then closes the door.

The driver-side door clicks in near-complete silence upon opening and shutting. Closed eyes pose no obstacle for me to sense his dominating presence, his ever-present aura. On any other date with any other man, the first questions of the night would've gone something along the lines of *How was your day?* or *Do you want to grab anything to eat?* A kiss, I would imagine, after the night we had.

Everyday stuff from everyday men. Much unlike Hudson is.

His right hand slips up my thigh, the car navigates silently through the city. "We're going somewhere no one can see what I'm about to do to you in and on this car."

The higher my skirt hikes, the harder it becomes to breathe. "I trust you."

"Good girl." He pushes his fingers up to my bare sex, stroking my entrance up and down. "You're dripping, Avery. You're fucking dripping, and I've barely touched you."

"Always." A moan swallows the single word I'm barely able to utter from the teasing of his finger as he pushes it a fraction deeper.

The car stops, and I hear the blinker clicking *click, click, click*. Two of Hudson's long fingers play with me, sinking and curling inside me, sliding the wetness up, pinching my swollen clit. My fingernails dig into my palm, my hips fight to stay put.

"Always what?" The noise from the blinker disappears and we're driving again.

Hudson is still rubbing me, stealing my air, and my ability to concentrate on anything other than the tantalizing pleasure he unleashes onto me.

"Wet for you," I hiss at the end of a gasp, adamant about giving him what he wants. "Always wet for you."

His touch is gone.

"Hudson?" I hesitate.

"Love your taste."

I squirm in my seat, the picture of his skilled tongue licking me off him too much to bear.

My seatbelt snaps open. Hudson's stubbled jaw after a long day at work tickles my cheek as he slides it off with care, his impressive weight inclining into me. "I didn't want to eat or drink today. Didn't want anything in my mouth that isn't your pussy. *My* pussy."

I'm a raging ball of energy, all of my senses other than sight straining with how badly I want Hudson on me. My reflexes kick in, snapping me out of being motionless, pressing my back forward.

Little Blue

It hurts everywhere, the profound desperation for a release.

One more touch, one more stroke.

Hudson presses his palm flat to my stomach, gliding it toward my chest. "Not yet."

The back of my seat suddenly inclines, and Hudson's breath is on me.

"As of today, I'm the exclusive owner of your pleasure, your screams, the multiple orgasms you can't take anymore." His expert fingers undo button after button of my shirt. The last button pops open, and Hudson draws it to either side, the heel of his palm caressing my stomach and beneath my breasts as he goes.

He's deliberately slow, dragging out this game for both of us. In his eyes, this isn't just an orgasm, me clenching around him isn't a record-setting mission to press the buzzer. It's an experience. He gets off on controlling me to the point my need to come is second in line after the need for him, behind my eagerness for his every praise.

"But you'll have to beg me for it, little." The tip of his tongue flicks my nipple.

A million nerve endings across my overstimulated body light up. It sears me everywhere, and a short scream bellows from me.

"Love that sound." Hudson's hot breath trails from one of my breasts to the other one.

"What if someone hears us?" The remaining focused cell of my brain manages to knock some sense into me.

"I told you, no," he quips, and then the tip of his tongue is on my right nipple, swirling around it, sinking his teeth into the hardened nub.

I scream out again, any concern about other people evaporates at the violent shock that spears me from where his mouth latches on me to my core.

"Hudson." His name mingles between short, desperate gasps inside the suffocating car.

"Your voice. I want to hear it." He removes his lips, resuming his taunting using one finger to circle my navel, dips it into the hollow space, then strokes it upward. "If you want anything from me, you better well say it."

A visceral growl rips from my throat when his finger slithers lower, patting my aching clit, before stopping. "Talk."

"I'm yours," I creak out the first thing that pops into my dazed mind. "I want you." He starts tapping again in a changing rhythm, and my head thrashes back. "I need you to let me come, Sir, please."

Hudson parts my lips, his hot breath heaving directly over my exposed flesh. "This. Pussy. Is. Mine. Say it."

Little Blue

I dig my heels deeper into the rug, panting, "My pussy is yours."

"You may come," he says, sucking my clit just as the words leave his lips.

A bright light hits me from the back of my eyes, illuminates the darkness Hudson's tie surrounds me with. I repeat his name, keep begging him for anything, I don't even know what, coming over and over, wave after wave, one quiver chasing the other.

But from the way Hudson keeps going at me, we're not even close to being done.

CHAPTER TEN
Hudson

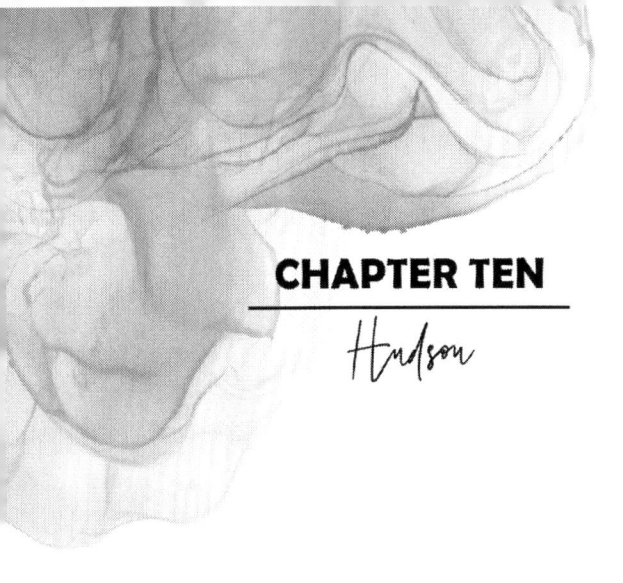

Avery unraveled against my hungry mouth, her soft thighs clenched around my face, pulling me further into her tight, young pussy, and fuck me if I don't want more of it.

To taste her, to imprint her scent to memory.

Play out the scenario I had planned for us.

I raise my head from her cunt to demand, "One more time, blue."

She shakes her head. "I can't."

Her shudders subside, all the tension in her body withers in tandem. She's pliant, melting into the chair, but very much like me, she wants more. It's evident in her quickened breath and how easily her legs part as I push them farther from each other.

"You have your word." I sink a finger in her soaking pussy. From there I go lower, spreading it on the rim of her other hole and applying the slightest pressure on that area. "You remember what it is?"

"Whit…"—moan—"…lock."

"Do you need it?" I lift my tie, cupping her jaw, and tilting her head so her eyes would meet mine under the soft glow of the park's streetlamps, to grasp the sincerity in them. "You won't disappoint me. You'll never disappoint me."

"No." She resurrects what little strength is left within her. "I take it back. I can."

"My little greedy slut." The blindfold returns to its place and I back to our roles. Straightening her seat, I order, "Do not move."

"Okay."

And to think I was turned on before when I saw my angel in black coming out to the lobby. She looked flawless; her cheeks rosy, the ponytail I've been yearning to pull from our days working together, the glimmering blue eyes I can spot in a crowd of a thousand people, it was all laid out for me to possess.

During the minutes she did me the honors by allowing me to touch her the way I craved, I wasn't simply sexually aroused. Something dormant was awoken, an unrivaled passion I have never felt.

Little Blue

In a heartbeat, I'm out of the car, closing the door behind me. I pat my jeans for the pink vibrator I bought for Avery, eager to use it on her. I reach her side, bending into a hugging position to untie the knot bounding her wrists, taking the opportunity to smell and nibble on whatever part of her I can reach.

She moans, my body reacting instinctively by shutting my eyes as it vibrates through me.

I can't get enough of her.

I fear I never would.

"Hold on to my neck."

Avery responds to my command, making it easier to scoop her in my arms. I drove us to the Golden Gate Park in front of where I live, pulling up to the side of one of the roads. Sometimes when I can't sleep late at night, I jog this route, which is how I knew it'd be secluded. It adds to the mystery, the smell of nature and fucking in an unconventional place such as my home. Something special. Like my girl.

I walk us to the back of the car, and when her bare butt comes in contact with the chilled black hood of the car, she flinches.

"Is that pretty ass cold?" I massage her thighs from the inside out, draping each foot on the hood and tossing her flats to the road beneath her.

"No." Her lips quirk in a smile, swaying her hips. "Feels kinda nice."

I shake my head, gathering she's talking about my touch rather than the car itself. And while I don't mean for her to be uncomfortable, in no way do I intend her to feel *nice*. I want her to experience what we're doing. I want her to appropriate the source of her soreness to me tomorrow, and every day after that.

Shoving myself between her legs, I wind her hair in my fist, tugging on it, forcing her chin up to the summer skies. My mouth is on her shoulder, sucking hard. "How about now?"

"You'll stop if I say better?"

"I'll stop *this* anyway." With a huff of a laugh, I draw out her hairband, relieving the pressure on her hair. "With you, though? Not in the slightest."

I grip her arms, keeping her secure as I twist her, helping her lie down. Avery's head is hanging low, her hands gripping my hips, her face directly at an eye-level with my crotch. Avery fucking Myers, clinging on to me, giving herself freely, her exposed form, bathed in the white-ashen lights from the streetlamps, is equally bare as her soul for me to take.

This image will follow me to the grave.

Little Blue

One of my palms moves from her arm up to where her fingers dig into my thighs. "Leave those there until I tell you otherwise. Can you do that for me?"

"Yes."

She sounds confident, trusting, and she has every reason to. I continue, hovering over her, fastening one palm on her naked stomach, the other on her toned calves. "Be a good girl and bend your knees."

Avery's movements are smooth, one leg bends after the other, her cute, blue painted toes planting into the metal of the car. "Like this?"

"Exactly like this." My fingers skim across her skin, teasing her clit, ending their travel on her stomach.

She breathes hard, each ebb and flow of her belly walloping through me. "Release now, blue."

The pressure of her grip is off me, and I hardly need to make any adjustments to the strength I apply to keep her in place. She's well-situated, allowing me to free a hand to undo my zipper. As I do, my gaze drifts from where our bodies connect to how her arms are floating, draped over the oceans of her long hair, then back to her breasts.

Before I drop my jeans to the floor, I yank out the vibrator, sealing it between my teeth. The rubber is both soft and firm, and I slip it from my mouth once my jeans and briefs hit the ground.

Eve Monks

My cock juts out, a drop of precum glistening at the tip. It throbs and aches for Avery, like my bones are, like my very soul is. I secure the vibrator in the hand that's holding her so I can bend a little and guide the head of my dick to her soft lips, smearing the moisture across them from corner to corner.

Avery surprises me by sending her tongue to taste the wetness on her.

My wetness.

Jesus fucking Christ.

"Listen to me carefully."

"Yeah," she hums, sounding dazed.

In a few seconds, and until my little one comes, she can be as spaced out as she wants to be. It's part of what pushes my pleasure buttons, so my girl will have it, but only after I give her a way out. Digging my fingers into her belly for attention, I say, "Listen to me, or the next orgasm you'll have will be in two weeks."

That is, whether you give me that long, I falter, eaten by the old doubt that has nothing to do with Avery, and everything to do with me. I snarl, refusing to entertain it longer than the second I already allotted to it.

She clears her throat. "I'm listening."

"Soon my cock will fill that delicate throat of yours." I fist myself tighter, picturing her hot mouth taking all of me. "In case you want me to slow down, tap twice, you want me to stop you tap once, and you make it loud. Got it?"

"Yes, Sir," she answers loud enough that I know the message came through.

"Now open wide."

I prod my shaft into her mouth the instant she does. My hand goes limp on Avery's belly, my teeth biting the inside of my cheek to keep from growling, from showing I lack any sort of restraint. Being in the position I am, as her leader, I can't afford to be anything else.

Her lips envelop me, and the slickness from the saliva pooling in her mouth makes sliding in and out of it a goddamn heaven. I thrust slowly, allowing her to adjust to my size while I flip the vibrator on with my thumb.

The pink device starts buzzing. Avery freezes, I assume from the unexpected noise and sensations.

"Relax your jaw." She does, and still, I worry any sudden, unfamiliar movement will scare her further. For her sake and my cock's sake, I clarify, "I have a toy I bought just for you."

When her tongue seeks out my cock, I give it to her, plunging a little deeper with each sway of my hips, my eyes rolling as I begin hitting the back of her throat.

"You're such a good girl." After I regain an ounce of my sanity, I finally talk, my voice cold and demanding.

"Taking me all in like that. Want your Sir to give you your reward?"

Avery moans, the vibrations raising the hairs on the back of my neck. On an impulse, I pound deeper. It's only this once, but I hear her choke, and feel more saliva dripping down my balls.

"Fuck, baby." I pause, waiting for my own tremors to run their course, gaining composure.

Instead of pounding into her again, I withdraw my cock somewhat, giving Avery air while gliding the vibrator over her belly, up to her breasts. The texture of her skin is pure silk, a contrast to the erectness of her nipples. I taunt the right one with the vibrator, patting it in pulses like I did to her clit.

She arches her head, trying to swallow my dick deeper. I brace myself from going too fast, too strong. "Slow. Down. You'll take what I tell you to, nothing more."

Her tongue traces circles on the crown of my cock, side to side over the shaft I push in slowly. "So good," I repeat the words to elevate her levels of arousal. "You're so fucking good."

The vibrator moves along her nipples in the rhythm I dictate, and I alternate it from one to the other. Twisting the hand on her belly so my fingers face her pussy, I drag it toward her pussy. I pound into her mouth twice then give her air while I curl my fingers inside her, resuming to pound her three more times as I rub and coat her clit with her juices.

The addictive scent of her cunt wafts up to me, her pink and glistening clit pleading to be pleasured by me.

Only me.

I slither the vibrator lower on her belly, assuming her tits are probably agonizingly aroused by now. The closer I glide the humming device toward her clit, the deeper I plummet into her. When I finally place it on her, applying pressure on her nub, turning it in circles, diving down, then back up, my girl lets out another, louder, guttural moan, so intense it reverberates to my very soul.

"Just like that, keep going." I plunge the moist vibrator deep into her wanting cunt, my other hand rubbing her clit roughly while I throat-fuck Avery with everything I have in me, only pausing momentarily to let her breathe. "Suck me off."

Between gags and moans, she hollows her cheeks, opens her throat for me to sink farther. She's so into what we're doing, into me, overwhelming me with love, lust, and gratitude. For years our relationship revolved around non-sexual gestures which gave me similar gratification, though nothing like this, like we're about to explode together.

And this mind-blowing contact is shared, bringing Avery to her second orgasm while I'm all over her. Avery's hips freeze in the air, then release to the hood of the car, her whole stomach rolling, body convulsing, her gasps for air becoming choked screams around my cock.

Having her satisfied drives me over the edge, and I follow her, releasing three bursts of my cum into her hot mouth. I pull out to allow her to swallow, switching off the vibrator and discarding it in favor of grabbing her hips and stabilizing her. With concise movements, I heft her back to a sitting position. Her feet dangle from my hood, her beautiful eyes remain hidden, a matter I amend once she's situated.

My tie cascades down her body, then to the ground. I stand between her thighs, curling my fingers around her throat, massaging it gently to soothe her, show her my profound appreciation. She arches her neck, clutching onto my gray T-shirt, dragging me to her.

"You took it so well." I slip my hands up to cup her cheeks, kissing her nose, looking directly into her eyes. They water, my words reaching to her as I meant them to.

"My beautiful, sweet girl," I add, eliminating what little distance is left between us, kissing her long and hard on her lips, refusing to give room for yesterday's doubts, from either of us.

Little Blue

But real life doesn't care for wishes, for the best motherfucking intentions.

Real life, as always, strikes you when you least expect it.

Avery returns the kiss, her nose nuzzles mine. "Thank you. Even though you don't mean it, thank you for saying it."

The shock has my eyes opening wide, glaring at her. "I do mean it."

She interrupts me, hurrying to say, "Calling me *yours*, Hudson. You don't know me, not really. You can't tell."

There we are, in the same place as yesterday. I get the sick heaviness in the pit of my stomach that it might be more than her guarding herself. That she's deflecting, when in reality she's the one who wants me for a casual fuck.

A filler, just like I was for my ex-wife.

I help her button-up, smooth over her skirt, turning from her. My shoulders slump, and I head to the car without waiting. "Come on, Avery. Let's get you home."

CHAPTER ELEVEN

Avery

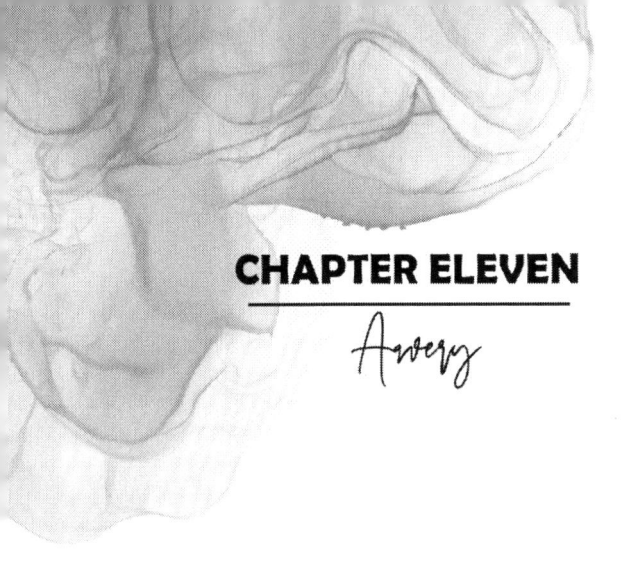

"Enjoy the weekend." I smile at my team. "Don't do anything I wouldn't!"

They chuckle, saying *Bye* back, and walk out together. I stuff my laptop into my bag plus the couple of catalogs Edna dropped off for me to go through over the weekend for our meeting on Monday, then grab my phone, checking the messages.

The last and only non-work-related text I received was from Jen about an hour ago, asking me if it's okay to bring Briar to our Friday night girls' date at *Robel's*. I don't mind the company, even though it's our *girls'* tradition. Briar is so good to my friend that I'm happy to have him join us.

Ever Marks

Kind of like I wish Hudson would've. I'm still beating myself up for what I told him three days ago, how my self-preservation trumped what my heart truly feels. When he touched me, cocooned me, claimed me as though I was his, I really was, and the man had a way to my soul like no other. How stupid was I to say he didn't know me?

With him, I belonged, I was loved, and I wanted to show my love for him in return. Which, in retrospect, was what scared the life out of me. This all-encompassing love, this unparalleled compatibility in every possible aspect that no one's ever come close to, it's too big, too scary. One of us had to break it.

My brain knows it. My heart, it still longs for that impossible love, and I can't stop staring at the phone, expecting a call from him. And I'm disappointed, even though what I suspected from the very start finally happened.

But I'll get over it. A couple or five cranberry vodkas and I'll be as good as new.

Sighing, I shoot Jen a message, saying *Of course*. I secure the strap of my bag to my shoulder, passing through the mostly empty offices and down the elevators, and out of the building. It's dark out, the sun having set an hour ago. I stand on the sidewalk near where I parked my bike, fluttering my eyes shut and wrapping my ponytail in my hand like I have the past three days.

Little Blue

The street noise ceases to exist.

The softness of a thin, expensive tie wraps around my head, covering my eyes.

You're such a good girl.

Heat spreads through me, surrounding me in the feel of Hudson. My breasts fit too snugly inside my mint-colored blouse, the crotch of my jeans suddenly too tight. My belly thrums, anticipation building.

Waiting for him.

Thank you, I imagine me saying. *I love you.*

What I'm doing isn't healthy, it won't make forgetting him any easier, yet I can't seem to help myself, can't stop craving him.

I open my eyes and…he's gone.

Hopping on my bike, I navigate my way through the city, averting my focus to the street, the people, and the end-of-the-week vibes of the city. The diversion distracts me from Hudson, which I'm grateful for, and by the time I hop off my bike outside the bar, I'm more than ready to drink, laugh, and basically wash away any sense of longing or dejection I've been dwelling on.

"Over here!" Jen waves at me the minute I step in.

She and Briar sit facing the entrance in our usual spot, at one of the red sofa booths placed on the side of the bar against the blue and white tiled wall. I wave back, strolling to them while bobbing my head to the song blasting from the speakers, *Gimme Some Lovin'* by The Spencer Davis Group.

"Hey." I slide inside the booth.

My arm hits someone. Apologies pour from me as I fix my bag off my shoulder and toss it in the free space beside me. "Sorry, I didn't see there was someone else here…"

Then his smell hits me, and it's too familiar to be considered any one of Jen's or Briar's friends.

It's Hudson. He occupies the space to my right, his charcoal-gray jacket that matches his slacks draped over by his side, his light-gray shirt rolled up, showcasing the accentuated veins on his arms. He glances down at me, a small smirk tugging at his lips, his green eyes sparkling.

"Hey."

Hey?! Hey?!

"We ran into a blast from the past," Jen prompts.

I can't look anywhere else except at Hudson. It's like, if I stare hard enough, my mind will eventually compute the why, how, and what the actual fuck he's doing here. To say I'm feeling a simplified emotion as a surprise would be a fucking joke. I'm a piñata stuffed with shock, rage, lust—and to top it all off—longing, so much so that I'm too stupefied to form a coherent response to either him or my friends.

Little Blue

"I hope it's okay." Hudson maintains a steady front, unwavering even when my face must portray the opposite of a welcoming expression. "I came here to drink, and Jen recognized me from some of your office party photos, I think?"

"Yeah," she chimes, her tone full of merriment. I stir myself from the trancelike state I'm in, turning to my friend so this situation won't get any more awkward than it already is. Jen slides over to me my cranberry vodka, which I leave unattended. "You had some group photos together, and I remember how much you loved working there."

Loved the old place, yes. Loved my team, my workspace, and the endless learning opportunities it offered. Most of all, though, I loved being around the man sitting next to me. Still do.

But no amount of love and adoration can compensate for three days of leaving me hanging. It's not like I couldn't pick up the phone to call him myself. I could. The whole point was to seek consistency from him, and sadly, he failed.

"Yeah, I have memories from almost everyone at Whitlock in my room," I mumble to appease Jen, then twist to Hudson. "There's actually something I forgot to pass on in training. Can we speak in private?"

I offer my friends an apologetic shrug. "Company secrets and all."

"After you." Hudson gestures with his hand to the outside of the booth. His long, talented fingers are in my line of view, a blatant reminder of the utmost sinful pleasures they inflicted on me. Each harsh knuckle, every pillowy fingertip. The man they're attached to.

Who isn't mine.

"When we come back, we'll continue our discussion about transitioning you to retail," Hudson addresses Briar as we unfold ourselves from the sofa.

"Thanks, man, I could use all the help I can get."

We head deeper into the bar toward the restroom area where there's a dark corner to talk in private. While we walk in silence, a tinge of sadness claws at my heart, because Briar has never told *me*, his friend who lives, breathes, and dreams of retail, that he's interested in switching his accounting job to a CPA firm.

Then again, Hudson has connections and is so easy to talk to.

I should know.

Whenever we'd finish the business we'd scheduled for our meeting ahead of time, Hudson would clear the work material from his desk, clasp his hands together and place his forearms on it, asking me how I was doing, showing interest in my life away from work. I'd tell him about my exams, my apartment hunting later, my after-work activities like chilling with Jen over a glass of wine and vodka on a Friday night…

Motherfucker.

I swivel swiftly once we're out of sight of the other patrons of the bar. The pink-orange LED cylinder behind me lights Hudson's smug face, his tall frame backing me to the wall. He slaps his hand on the wall over my head, bracketing me to the black wall, lowering his head to mine.

My breath hitches in my throat as my back hits the wall. "You remembered."

"Is that your way of saying you're happy to see me?" He laces playfulness into the question, ignoring the existence of these three days we were apart.

"Fuck, Hudson, you know I am." I huff, dropping my gaze from his eyes in a dire attempt to save myself from getting lost in him again. "Like I would've been any of the last few days."

"Little girl, did you just talk back to me?" He slips into the other voice. *That* voice.

Its potency weakens my knees, ignites a fire in my lungs.

But hiding in my obedient space, giving in to the desires we both blatantly burn in, will only enable him to continue his behavior of toying with my emotions. Every fiber of my being wants to be with him, to form a deeper, more meaningful connection than sex.

And in order to have me, in any capacity, he should crave it, too.

I raise my chin in defiance, summoning courage, looking him square in the eyes. "I won't play games, because I don't like being played. So, let's be clear, Hudson. What made you come for me when it's been so convenient to act like I don't exist?"

The next thing I know, his hand grips my hair, his body pinning me into the wall. "You. Only ever fucking you."

CHAPTER TWELVE
Hudson

$\mathcal{A}$very didn't mean what she said the other day. Not how I interpreted it, anyway.

It's obvious in the misstep in her confident tone, in the hurt she tries to seal behind those clear blue eyes of hers. I see her, I truly see her.

And after I've had days to get over my pathetic self, I'm here to obliterate the doubts out of her as well. The nice approach didn't work. Talking is out of the question. My little blue will just have to understand how much I'm into her the hard way.

"Today, maybe, but yesterday? The day before that? Was it *only ever* Rina that you went to when you weren't talking to me?"

Especially when she's acting like a brat. I pull Avery's hair harder so she's glancing up, looming over her face, filling her view with the one who's in control, who she'll answer to because he's the one who cares the most.

"No." I grind my dick on Avery, showing her what she and no one else does to me. "But I like that you're jealous."

Her teeth snap over her plump bottom lip as a whimper nearly escapes her. "I'm not."

I graze her with my lips, traveling from her chin to her ear. "Seems awfully lot like jealousy from where I'm standing."

"I can't believe you." When I lick the inside of her shell, she gives out the tiniest sigh, so I go on, listening to her as I go. "You said I'm yours, then you disappeared."

"You are mine, I just…"

"Yours to fuck, you mean."

My head snaps up, my hand releases her by an inch. My forehead presses to hers, and I growl, "No."

"Yours to hide."

The mouth on her. "No."

"Yours to bring out of the toy box whenever you're inspired for some rough sex."

"Avery…" I call her given name, implying I'm really starting to get pissed off.

Little Blue

"Hudson." The disobedience slowly slips away from her glare, morphing into a shade of sadness. "Why won't you make it easy for me to accept what happened and admit that's all we have? Just sex?"

Wherever she stumbles, I must be strong. I steel my voice, saying, "Because it'd be a lie. I…"

"For three years, three stinking years, I've done everything to show you I'm interested," she hisses. "Smiled, shared my personal life, gave you priorities over my own boss."

"You think I haven't noticed?" is my sole response as anger simmers into my blood, resentment mostly toward myself. I should've risen above my insecurities and talked to her like a mature adult much earlier.

And I hate myself even more, because she extends that generosity to me, opening up, explaining what I've done wrong. Avery steps up, and despite her age, she shows me she's braver than I am. And me, thirteen years her senior, I'm not nearly as close to being this courageous.

"You had to have been blind to miss them." She deflates slowly before my eyes, and her diminished spirits stick the knife deeper into my chest. "That's my issue, why I didn't believe the *You're mine* declaration even before you went AWOL on me. What an idiot I am. A thirty-seven-year-old man, the CFO of one of the largest beverage companies in the US, you never thought of me as anything but a temporary amusement, a means to fulfill your dominant fantasies. You were too scared I'd stir shit as a random fuck in the office, but now, now that I'm out of your territory, you can come piss on me whenever you feel like."

"You're much more than that." Avery purses her lips, refusing me when I inch lower to kiss her. I sigh, my heart aching, my role getting continuously harder to hold on to. "I crashed your girls' night to tell you I do care. I always did."

Tears prickle the corners of her eyes. They aren't there due to the tug on her locks, the pressure of my front on hers. I'm provoking her to tread on a dangerous ledge, the physical exertion proving too much combined with the emotional baggage my fierce woman is carrying.

My concern for her overpowers my wishes to keep her with me, listening to my explanations. I ease off her fast, unfastening my fingers from her hair. "Avery, I'm sorry."

She sidesteps me, waiting for me to turn around to say, "Prove it, Hudson, and I'm yours."

With a sad quirk of her lips, spins on her heels and walks out, disappearing as I remain there baffled as to how one little girl could be so fucking right.

CHAPTER THIRTEEN
Avery

"Dude, you missed out on such a great night." Jen hugs me from behind while I pour myself my second coffee this morning, giving me a quick peck.

"Yeah, we were hoping to hang out together," Briar adds. "Hudson left right after you, though he did give me his number. I get why you liked it there so much."

"Yes, he really is great," I lament. "I'm sorry for bailing, it's been one of those weeks and suddenly everything caught up to me."

My excuse sounds lame to my own ears, so I busy myself instead of giving off any more hints of my bluff. From the cupboard above me, I pull out two mugs, pour the hot liquid into them, then pass them to Jen and Bri to add sugar and cream.

"Thanks," she says, fixing their drinks. "We actually had a surprise for you."

The declaration tears me from my avoidance attempts. I raise my eyes to my roommate. "You mean another surprise, if you're not counting my ex-coworker."

Jen leans her hip on the counter with Briar to her right, twirling the spoon in her mug, a wicked grin marking her face. "Not as hot as Hudson, but—"

"Hey!" Briar hugs her side, nuzzling the top of her head affectionately. "He's my friend."

"Samuel is for sure sweet, don't get me wrong. Sweet like cuddle-me-by-the-campfire, sweet." She wags her eyebrows at me. "Hudson is…well, he seems the kind of man to flip you on his lap and spank you until it's red and raw and you scream for Daddy, i.e., him."

Heat flares across my neck, my ears, my cheeks. I haven't met this Samuel person, but Jen's description of Hudson couldn't be more dead-on. I mean, the distance between Sir and Daddy isn't far, seeing how in the time we spent together, he enveloped me in that sense of being guarded, looked after, cared for, and…

And why am I even entertaining these notions? It's not like he chased me, or called. It's pointless.

"I thought you liked cuddles." Briar's hand trails down to Jen's waist, tickling her.

Little Blue

"I do." Her giggles fill our little kitchen as she leans deeper into her boyfriend. "All I'm saying is, you gotta acknowledge the facts for what they are."

Briar's tickling intensifies, each of his kisses turning this scene a little less friendly by the second, which is adorable. Also, it's my ticket out of this awkward conversation.

"I'll be in my room if you need me. Although something tells me you won't." I hide a smile, steering toward the open door.

"Avery," Briar's kind voice brings me to a halt, and I look over my shoulder at him. "What about another day? Give Sam a shot?"

I bite the inside of my cheek, uncertain how to respond to his question without coming off as condescending since I obviously can't say my heart belongs to someone else.

"Um, I..."

The phone in my sleep shorts pocket beeps four times one after the other, saving me from giving Briar an immediate answer. "One sec, it might be a work emergency."

Jen starts protesting, something along the lines of my boss and lack of boundaries when I pull out my cell.

Hudson: *You've been a bad girl, blue.*
Hudson: *Mouthing off, running like that yesterday.*

Eve Monks

Hudson: *Go to your room right now.*

Hudson: *Get on your hands and knees and FaceTime me when you're there.*

This isn't what I had in mind when I told him to prove his commitment to me. I deserve love, conversations resembling those Hudson and I held three short months ago, constant attention before jumping back to sex.

Trying not to get sucked into uncalled-for drama, I close my eyes, regroup, and read it anew.

Hudson of the past week introduced me to another side of him. He caught me each and every time I stumbled, delivering me to safety with his imposing voice and harsh touches. Writing me these things is his way to put me in the headspace where I know he's heard me, he's present, he's holding the ball I tossed at him, making the effort I urged him to.

"Urgent." I open my palms facing up in apology to Briar, then turn to my room. "We'll talk later."

"Want to join us for breakfast?" Jen asks.

Raising my mug, I talk behind a half-closed door. "All set, thanks. I'll probably head out to the office, so go, have fun. We'll watch a movie or something in the evening."

"Okay…"

I ignore the skepticism in her tone, clicking the lock behind me. Following Hudson's orders, I lower myself to the floor, hands and knees on my rug. The action by itself,

Little Blue

the obedience, succumbing to his will, blows up a bubble of endorphins in my body. They swarm through my bloodstream, a mixture of arousal and belonging for which I have to close my eyes because the high it carries with it is just so. Incredibly. High.

I reach for the AirPods on my nightstand, place them in my ears, dialing his number. While the phone rings, I place it between my hands, below my head, and wait.

And wait.

And wait.

It's a form of punishment for not calling him right away, another link to connect us, to make me realize I'm so important to him that I need to remember to return his messages faster next time. I accept it, I cherish it, I bask in it even as I wait.

His commanding presence is everywhere, from the rug beneath me to the air I breathe.

He's ruined me for all other men.

"My little blue."

He appears on the screen wearing a black T-shirt. The dark blond hair he usually keeps tidy is mussed, light scruff grazing his jaw, his lips pinched tight.

A shrill runs up my spine, my breasts weighing heavy with lust. I bite my bottom lip, searching for my voice. "Sir."

Ever Marks

"You hurt me last night. Saying those things." His tone is steady, unlike the rampant beats of my heart. "Leaving me like that."

"I did."

"You did what?"

"I did all of the above, Sir."

He moves the phone to the side, perching his jaw with his other hand, tapping his index finger to his cheek. "Is there anything else?"

Seeing his formidable face, I hesitate, considering asking for forgiveness and having it done and over with. I breathe, remembering I've come so far, I said my piece yesterday, and if the type of relationship I'm after doesn't suit him, it's better we end this now.

"No." I shake my head subtly, my long tresses swing from left to right.

Light passes through his eyes, a flash and it's gone. Darkness takes over as he leans forward, quirking up a sardonic eyebrow. "You're not sorry?"

He's not in the room, yet I feel his arm around my throat, its strength and sensuality as he chokes me.

"No. I want you to myself, for the long haul, or nothing at all."

"But was that the way to talk to me?"

"That was the only way I had."

Little Blue

"All right." He exhales slowly, a gesture meant to signal exasperation. "We're going to play a game, you and me. First, sit back on your heels, move the camera over your body so I can see what you're wearing."

Butterflies plague my stomach from the prospect of being watched by him. I follow his order, trailing the phone from my bare knees and thighs, up to my white shorts and my oversized ocean-blue T-shirt.

"Show me what's under your shirt." He almost looks bored when I flash him my white bra. "Go lower."

I angle the camera lower until my matching boy shorts appear on the screen, raising my hips to remove them.

"Pants stay on. You'll do well to remember who owns you, blue, and you won't do anything without my permission." He relaxes back again.

Hudson changes the hands holding the phone, reaching below with his free one out of his camera's reach. He doesn't have to tell me where it's going, though, how he's fisting his large cock, rubbing the silky surface.

And as much as I'd love to see it, I don't ask him for it. The subtle hint, the teasing of it, it only serves to make it that much hotter.

This is one punishment I can get behind.

"Put the phone away. I want to see your profile when you go on all fours."

I rest it against the nightstand, arranging myself to present him the angle he asked for. His strong arm slides up and down in languid strokes while I sit there, ogling him.

"Two fingers in your mouth, I want them wet." He groans as I shove them inside. "Suck on them."

The penetration of my fingers and the act of hollowing my cheeks and sucking on them send me to the evening Hudson's cock then cum filled my mouth, and my eyes flutter shut on their own.

"Eyes open. I didn't say you could look away." He ensnares my gaze, even from far away. "Your fingers soaked?"

I let them drop on my bottom lip, dragging it lower. "Yes, Sir."

"Your pussy?"

My head bobs up and down.

"What did we say about words, Avery?" His breaths are shallow, his hand movements a tiny bit faster. "Speak."

"My pussy is soaked." I barely breathe, the cloud of arousal expanding in my lungs. "For you."

His smirk is instant. "As it should be. Now I'm going to guide you on how to fuck that tight, soaking cunt."

"Thank you." Relief takes over, and I slide them to the waistband of my shorts, pushing them beneath the garments to my aching clit.

Little Blue

He chuckles, a rough, clipped sound. "Don't thank me just yet. Are they in?"

"Yes." I'm barely holding myself upright, they're so deep.

"Good girl." He pauses whatever he does, putting the phone down to whip his shirt off, revealing ridges of taut, hard planes I want to have my tongue over. "Don't stop because of me. Stroke your clit, use your thumb."

I'm rolling my hips, unsure whether the physical touch, Hudson's undivided attention, or watching him pleasure himself is what stirs me closer and closer to an orgasm. I bite my tongue, stifling moans from reaching Jen and Briar, rocking faster on the rug.

"Take the middle finger out of your cunt and dip it in your ass."

My trust in him is so obsolete, I do as he says, even though no one or nothing has ever gone in there. It feels weird, and my face twitches at the uncomfortable pressure.

"Keep your hips moving,"—he instructs, when a hungry growl tears through him,—"make small circles with the finger, relax into it."

Hudson's authority and guidance help as I probe myself a little deeper.

"Good girl," he comments when my face contorts under a tsunami of pleasure I've yet to experience.

Ever Mine

The gentle tissues stretch and expand. The hint of pain similar to the raw spanking Hudson subjected me to. I feel touched, feel his presence at my back, his hot breath on my neck egging me on.

"Oh. My. Fuck," I breathe out, my lower hand grips the rug, nails diffing into the fibers.

"Don't come. Do. Not. Fucking. Come."

I stop completely. I have to. I recognize my body's signals as much as Hudson does over the phone. The coiling in my stomach, the slight shiver of my thighs—I'm practically there, and I want to be so good for him.

Hudson's eyebrows knead together. "Did you hear me say you can quit?"

In the distance, I hear *Bye, Avery*, then the door slam.

"Hudson, my friends left. I'm so lonely in this big room." My voice sounds whiny, but I'm beyond the point of caring. Hudson delivered me to the door of desperation, literally on my knees and begging for my big man, for his body, for the relief I'm craving.

"I'm not coming. But maybe I'll decide to allow you to." He tilts his head.

"What?" I pant. My sex clenches, the ache of holding off mounting to intolerable levels.

"Let's try this on for size. You said you're not sorry earlier." One of his eyebrows arches. "Are you sorry for last night? For dropping me when I showed up to have a nice evening with you? To ask that you forgive me for taking too long to sort myself and tell you how much I want you?"

Hudson's candor is almost palpable, constricting my chest with regret. On the other hand, it's not like he announced it. I won't be guilted for protecting my heart. I drop my hand, falling to my knees. "Your dick grinding on me doesn't give off I'm sorry vibes."

"Avery Myers, I get fucking hard for you. I got hard for you every time you so much as uttered my name on your luscious lips, thinking what my dick would look like wrapped by them." He inches toward the screen, green, endless meadows of his eyes plowing into my soul. "Doesn't take away from what I feel. From how I fought Andrew to give you that job you deserved without making my personal feelings obvious. From the two guys I threatened to fire for saying inappropriate shit about you."

My mouth slacks, my bottom lip drops. He hasn't told me any of it, and now that I know, it throws me into a whole other realm. I'm an emotional mess, too stupefied to either think or speak.

"I didn't do it to win points with you. Shit. You weren't meant to hear about any of it." He huffs a long sigh, eyes cast low then up to meet me again. "You said I should've known you liked me. I guess I hoped you realized it was mutual."

"Hudson."

The shift in his expression is immediate. The slip of softness is devoured by steel gaze, a tick of his jaw. "You didn't though, but soon I'm going to make it so you can't forget. You'll be on the brink of an orgasm for however long I instruct you to, so this moment will be ingrained thoroughly into your subconsciousness whenever insecurities rise. You'll remember your struggle, and you'll remember these words, little—I'm falling for you. I'm all yours."

He's silent, allowing the information to sink in. I believe it, his sincerity is undeniable.

"You get it, don't you?" His tone inclines toward forgiveness, if only for a moment.

"Yes."

"Good girl." He reclines on the couch, his arm begins swaying again on the screen. He's in control, demanding, a picture of seduction. My fluffy emotions of love and butterflies wither away, my blood rushing to my cunt.

"Put on your shoes, pack a change of clothes, then get on your bike to ride to the home address I'll text you. Next time, any time, I'd come for you. Now, your sensitive pussy will have to endure the jolts and vibrations

Little Blue

of the ride, to hold onto your orgasm until you're with me."

He hangs up at that, leaving me to bathe in the anxiety and exhilaration. Hudson's right and I trust him to ask me what'll benefit the both of us as a couple.

A couple.

We'll have to open that discussion, after more truths from the both of us.

When we're both sated and clothed.

I don't waste another second, scurrying to my feet and rushing to the man I crave more than anything in this world.

CHAPTER FOURTEEN
Hudson

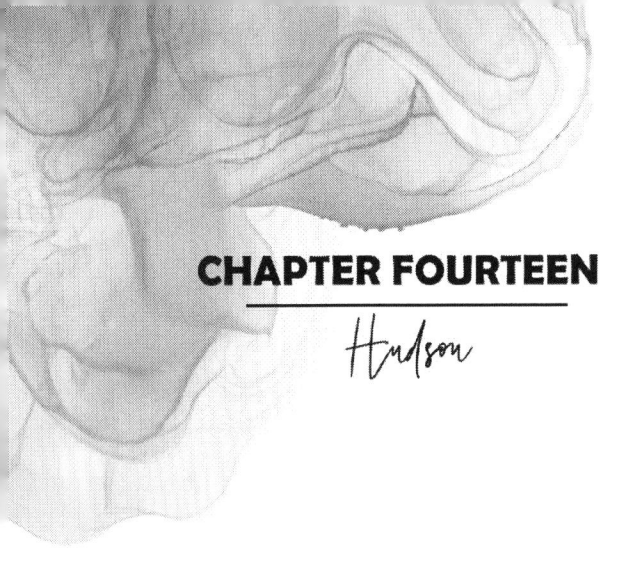

I walk around the house, drawing the blinds, preparing for Avery's arrival.

My sweet, little blue has every reason to demand to be more than a means to blow off steam. After I'll fuck the tension out of her and myself, break the both of us then piece ourselves back together, I'll hold on to her. I'll cherish her, be a partner to her and won't let go; regardless of how many times she'll tell me our relationship won't work.

I'll be mentally strong and exhibit equal poise as I do physically.

Because I'm crazy about her, and I'm done running away.

Ever Marks

The doorbell rings just when I shut the last blind in the living room. I traverse through it, pacing into the foyer of my Mediterranean Revival home on my bare feet, my breaths strained the less distance there is between us.

My hand hovers above the doorknob of the wooden carved door, stretching the anticipation a minute longer. When I finally pull on the door, I'm confronted with a set of wide blue eyes. They're hungry, desire pouring from them, yet Avery gives nothing in her body language. Her spine is erect, her mouth clamped shut, her arms at her sides.

Blood swells my cock, tenting my gray sweats. I clear the way for Avery. "Get in."

She leaves her bike parked outside in my driveway, taking a step into my home and stopping, her white sneakers glued to one another. So are her thighs.

I round her to the door, slamming it shut. Standing behind her, I plaster a hand on top of her mouth, snaking the other arm to the front of her body, forcing her to my chest.

"I love your smell." My nostrils flare as I inhale the scent of sleep and sweat and sex, grinding myself against her body, relieving the edge I can't shake off without her.

"Thank you," she mumbles, her eyes unblinking.

"Into the living room," I instruct after the ache in my cock dulls by a fraction.

Little Blue

Avery walks, matching her steps to mine. She allows me to manhandle her onto all fours like I watched her kneel on our FaceTime call. To experience her in the flesh though is riveting—the tips of her hair grazing my Persian rug, her ass pinned to my throbbing erection, my arm around her breasts—it's enough for me to come on the spot.

But if I'm not in control, she's all over the place, too. I slide one hand from her mouth to her hair, grasping it, pulling hard while draping it away from her ear.

Bending down, my lips brush it while I whisper, "Were you a good girl on the ride here?"

"Yes, Sir." The caress of her hair on my stubbled cheek feels like feathers, soft and lush.

"I'm about to check, so you better not be lying to me."

She doesn't reply when my fingers drift down her body and under her shorts. The pad of my middle finger connects with the taut mound.

A shout, very similar to that I heard in my car pierces my ear.

It's the sweetest sound, that of obedience. Of holding back, of accepting me as her guide, her Sir. And I'd do anything, even jump off the Golden Gate Bridge, rather than disappoint her.

"You're handling what I give you so well." I connect my index finger to my thumb, flicking her clit as my teeth close on her earlobe. She whimpers, groaning louder when I release her. "And if you'll be a good girl and do as I instruct you, I'll forget all about last night. I'll make you scream my name so that pretty throat of yours wouldn't be able to say anything else throughout the weekend."

I don't wait for her reply, straightening up on my knees and spreading her legs wider apart. Her nails dig deeper into my rug when I wind her T-shirt in my hand, pulling it up her waist. Her shorts and panties are pulled down next.

"Show me what you did at home."

"Not if you don't want me to come."

I lift my hand in the air, and in the complete silence from both the house and the street, my palm meeting her cheek makes the sound of the first thunder of a storm. Repeating the action, I slap her a second time on the same, burning spot, robbing her of the smallest moment to recuperate.

"Hold yourself." My command is as much of a whip as my smacks on her round behind when she stumbles forward.

"I can't, I…" She turns her head to me, eyes watery though free from pain. "I almost came."

Little Blue

"You can, blue. You're mine, and you'll do whatever I tell you to."

Another slap rings in our ears after all she does is shake her head.

I massage the bright red area, the reddening from my spanking prominent under the thin strips of light permeating through the blinds. Then I land another series of strikes, one for each word. "I am not asking again."

Avery's arms tremble, the heightened arousal plaguing her infects me the same. My clothes tighten on my skin, a thin layer of sweat coats the muscles of my back.

"Move it." Flattening my palm on the curve of her spine, I drag it lower, covering the unhurt butt cheek menacingly, although I'm aware she loves the pain I inflict, yearns for it.

However, not as much as she craves pleasing me. Avery lifts her fingers to her cunt, the connection coaxing a shaky breath from her. She sways, then removes a finger to reach her butt. I watch and listen and absorb her, mesmerized. And I've had my fill of being the observer.

I suck on my thumb, spitting on it, and slap her hand away from her butt. "Keep pleasuring your pretty wet pussy." I sink my thumb up to the knuckle. The spit from both her and me and how fucking relaxed she is, make it easy to plunge it deeper every time. "I'll take care of you from behind."

Ever Mine

She does just that, moans, and holds her breath in intervals, attempting to stay with me. My admiration for her is blinding, my need to make love to her consumes me. I pull out my thumb slowly, grab her hips, flip her, resting her back on the rug.

She eyes me, searching for clues she might've done something wrong.

"You did so well." I gaze down at her, making sure she realizes she didn't disappoint me. "But I want to be inside of you."

She smiles, and it's the most beautiful thing I've seen. I dive into her lips, devouring her. Our tongues explore one another, and she tastes like heaven, like she's mine.

"Have you been tested?" My question comes out as a growl when I press my shaft further to her warmth, feeling her wetness soak through my sweats.

"Yeah," she gasps between dire kisses, our lips barely separating. "On the pill, too."

She doesn't have to say another word. I reach back to shrug out of my pants and boxer briefs. Avery's determined feet help relieve me of them completely, while I yank down her bra, exposing her breasts.

The detonative field of electricity in the air we share buzzes loudly, blaring out the sounds of our labored breaths, of Avery's gulp from the dip of the head of my cock into her pussy. Her pebbled nipples arch higher as she pushes up to get me in deeper.

"Greedy little slut." I slap her breasts, then bend low to put one of her tits in my mouth to suck on at the exact moment I thrust my cock into her. In one thrust, I shove inside, biting Avery's hard mound with the tornado of emotions wracking my body and heart.

"Hudson, please." She tears at my hair, her thighs trembling around me. "I can't, I can't."

I bracket her agonized face with my forearms. My thrusts into her are slow, determined to prolong it for her. "I'm crazy about you."

"M-hmm." Her eyes are like the view of a summer's sky, the tears from fighting her most basic instinct are like early morning's dew.

One, round drop spills down her reddened cheek and my lips catch it, tasting the brine, the divinity, the promises in it.

"And I'll keep coming back for you." Every inch of her stretches with each plunge, but she's still so tight. "Unless you absolutely can't stand the sight of my face, I'll be back for you. I'm not letting go."

Her hands search for a grasp on my cheeks again, and I evade them. "Tell me you understand, tell me you'll do the same."

Ever Marks

"I do." She rolls her eyes from my rough shove. I'm still, waiting for her to look at me. She does, new strength ingrained in them. "I do. And I will."

I press my forehead to hers, her eyes are everything I see. "You have my permission. Come for me."

Before I even finish the sentence, her walls tighten, her heels digging into my ass, coercing me to fill her up with every inch of me. We're glued, my body absorbing her tremors, my eyes inhaling the ecstasy coursing through hers.

Tears upon tears of relief drench her hair, and I kiss their trail, kiss her temples, her ears, fucking her for all that I'm worth.

"Blue," I ground out her name, repeating it as my own orgasm hammers in my chest, rocks my stomach, ending in my cock. I hug her, nuzzling her neck and breathing out the only word I remember now. "Blue."

CHAPTER FIFTEEN
Avery

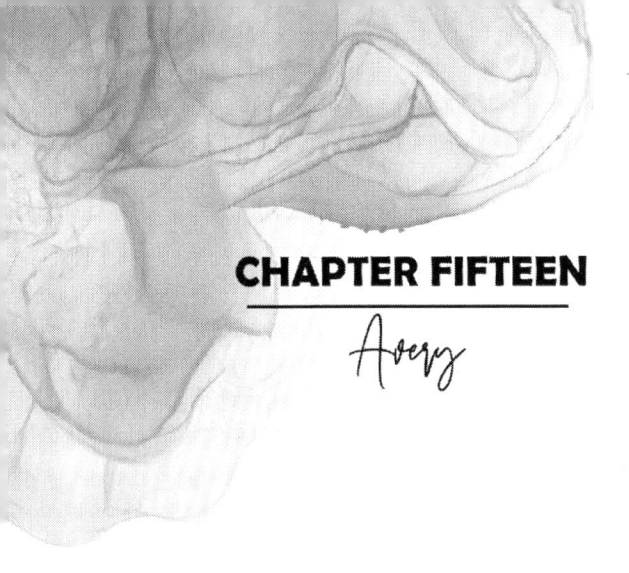

"Blue," I hear Hudson sigh my name in my ear.

I hear him, I'm comforted by him and the commitment we've declared.

Yet I can't seem to stop crying.

He's still inside me, his face is buried in my hair, lips in my neck, stubble on my cheek. I kiss his temple, encapsulating him in my arms, hugging his broad shoulders, feeling the rich fabric of his T-shirt beneath my palms as they glue him to me.

When Hudson's breaths resume their regular pace, he lifts on his lean forearms, worry creasing his smooth forehead. "Why are you crying?"

Overpowered by emotions, words escape me and I draw him closer. His green eyes clear through the lingering silence, his body tenses from the evolving concern.

"I'm not sad, I'm more…pacified," I murmur, the sensation of being not-here-nor-there preventing any form of coherent speech.

"Avery."

The unrelenting cadence of his voice brings me to the present, a tight grip on my arm to catch me as I freefall aimlessly into my emotions. But with him, life makes sense again.

I blink, my chest expanding against Hudson's clothed one. "I'm here. I'm okay. Thank you."

His swollen lips quirk to the side, a twitch, before returning to his somber, soothing expression. He kisses my forehead, slides to the side, then proceeds to handle me with the utmost care. I watch enchanted as Hudson fixes my bra, pulls my shirt down my stomach, and my shorts over my hips.

He swoops me up, his pace and hold are as strong as they are tender.

Kids run outside on this late Saturday morning, a ball hopping on the pavement, a faint cooking scent flooding Hudson's house.

And I am his.

"Here we go." He settles us into the sand-colored loveseat facing the elegant fireplace in the minimalistic living room. I'm in his lap, my hands slack around his neck, my heart comforted by the way Hudson's thumb runs reverently across my cheek, though the flow of my tears has dried by now.

After he studies my face for any other signs of non-existent distress, his approach reverts to the soft protector. Gently, he pries my fingers from behind his neck, brushing his lips on my palms where light abrasions caused by the gripping of the rug appear. "I'm going to get you some tea, rest for a bit, then we'll talk."

The shadow of a smile I offer him soothes him further, and he lifts me slightly to place me on the cushions. The soothing weight of his gaze follows me as he unfolds from the cozy sofa, his hand passing along my head down to my chin.

"Can I bring you anything else?"

"A blanket?" Suddenly, even a moment without him sends a cold chill down my spine despite the warm weather.

With one firm nod, he turns to the armchair, swaddling me in a white throw blanket, and as though he can't resist himself, he bows to my nose, giving me a quick peck.

My eyes flutter shut, my heart resorting to its regular pace. During the short minutes Hudson's gone, I rearrange my thoughts, reverting to the questions I had while I was home, summoning the courage to discuss the meaning of a relationship when the fog of hormones doesn't make me want to jump him, to hell with consequences.

"There." The cushions dip lower with his weight.

I open my eyes to two mugs of steaming tea sitting on a wooden end table and a fully dressed Hudson. "I didn't even hear you coming."

He threads his fingers through my hair, tucking a loose strand away. "You were pretty out of it."

"What? But you just sat here."

"You were sleeping when I walked in. At peace. Didn't seem right to disturb you." His somber mien creaks, his pinched lips suppressing a smile. "Could be I just stood and watched you for a while."

Any other person doing that would've freaked me the fuck out. But this man, the guy I get butterflies from, my enamored heart wishes I could replay it somehow and see it. Stunned by the flood of emotions, I only smile.

He brings one cup to his lips, blows on it gently, then passes it on to me. "I remembered you liked Earl Grey. One sugar. Right?"

My outfits, and now my tea choice. If there's been a shred of hesitation of the fact that his care is sincere earlier, it's gone out the window. "For how long?"

"How long what?"

Little Blue

"How long have you..." I sip from the mug, masking the blush spreading on my cheeks. "Liked, um, me. Or you didn't. I don't know. Fuck. Why is this so awkward?"

He tilts his head, freeing his playful smile for my eyes to feast on. "You're adorable."

"Glad my unease amuses you."

"I said you're adorable." I give him my cup when he reaches for it. Once it's settled on the table, Hudson scoops me into his lap, lies on the arm of the sofa, arranges the blanket on top of me, and brings his mouth to my shoulder. "Beautiful, too. You and your honesty. I envy you, how you unabashedly ask what's on your mind. It doesn't come that easily for me."

This powerful, successful man who runs an entire company that doesn't move either left or right unless *he* okays it, who's been the youngest in Whitlock's one-hundred years to occupy the CFO position, is intimidated to speak his mind to *me*.

I don't think so.

"Hudson." I twist to face him, pinning his gaze to mine, and lowering my eyebrows in a faux-serious expression. "Besides making me swear I'm yours, you mentioned—I think—the names of all of my privates, called me a slut, and..."

My speech is cut short, Hudson's fingers digging into my waist, sending me rolling in laughter. "Brat."

"I'll start, then," I manage when he finally ceases the brutal attack. I snuggle into his chest, resting my head on it. "I liked you the minute you entered our office."

"Did you? What made you like me?"

At last, I'm the surprised party.

"I can pick at it, say it was your eyes, your lips, your perfect hair, your hot body in a suit, your swagger." I pause, staring at the arched pathway in front of us. "It was all and none of them, though. It was you. Just you."

His hands roam up my belly, teasing the bottom of my bra. "If I'd have realized it would've taken you to leave the company to say these things to me, I would've found a cause to fire you myself three years ago."

"Three?" The shock dries my mouth, every syllable stretched out. I spin my head to meet his once more, needing to affirm he's not fucking with me. Pools of honesty and apprehension are mirrored in his green gaze, not a drop of a lie in them. "You're serious."

"This"—he motions his finger between us—"is mutual. From the first second I laid my eyes on you."

"I have so many questions." I fully turn to lay on him belly-to-belly, face-to-face.

A thin strip of sunlight prevails through the slant the curtain doesn't cover. The golden stroke highlights the side of Hudson's face, making him even more striking. But as enchanted as I feel, my curiosity prevails.

Little Blue

"You never said anything, how come?"

His chest rises, then falls, speaking without a hint of condescension. "The world isn't black or white. You'll get it when you're older."

"Oh, please, thirteen years is nothing."

He cocks an eyebrow, his lips twisting into a rueful smile. "You passed the drinking age around the time you started working with us, you're not even twenty-five yet. That's a year younger than I should date sign if I ever saw one."

"Fuck off."

"That mouth." Hudson's groan precedes him pinching my lips, kissing me into oblivion.

His cock hardens against my belly, and he stops kissing me. He listened to what I asked, fully intending to talk. Wanting nothing more than to hear him out, I push myself up to cuddle to his side, squishing against the side pillows. Our legs entangle, our arms find each other in an embrace.

"You must've heard about my divorce." He continues when I bob my head once in agreement, "It was finalized less than a month before I even knew you existed. And by then, I wasn't in love with her, nor was she with me. She…"

A heavy sigh hijacks the flow of his speech, his eyes avoid me. "She's not a bad person. I guess we'd outgrown each other, fell out of love after dating since high school. I spent way too many hours at work, and the few hours I was at home, I wasn't really there, you know?"

I bite the inside of my cheek, understanding firsthand the price of ambition, the little to no energy remaining by the end of the day.

"She went to find love in other places. With another man who could give her what I couldn't." He shrugs, playing it off when his eyes portray a whole other story.

A hot rod of rage sears me. I open my mouth to point out she wasn't as innocent, and Hudson quiets me with a kiss.

"Don't. The past is in the past, I didn't tell you about it to upset you." His warm palms cradle both sides of my face. "I'm trying to explain why it's hard for me to trust. Why I procrastinated, why our communication felt safe from afar, and why it took losing you for me to wake the fuck up. But I realized over the months you were at your new job and over the three days I hid like a coward that a future without you isn't a future at all."

The sadness in the air around him is palpable, though I don't think it's because of his ex. Not anymore.

"Thank you for confiding in me, for helping me understand your motives." I place a hand flat on his chest. "It lights everything differently. I knew you were attracted to me, but when for three years you contained it, never said a word, I figured it was purely sexual. I followed the logic that a serious relationship wouldn't be perceived badly around the office, while a sexual one, had it gotten out, would trash your reputation, so you left it at that. I'm so sorry I misjudged you."

"Avery." My name is both reverence and remorse on his lips. "That's a part of the reason I held back, too."

"Which part?" Confusion hit me, along with a dire attempt to avoid jumping to conclusions.

"I didn't want people talking about you. For your sake, your career. Your ambition, your hard work, the genius you are." He's quick to reassure me. "Gossip and jealousy would've cheapened it, whether we announced a serious relationship or were two adults having casual, consensual sex. They'd say you're fucking your way to get ahead."

My brow raises, and he squeezes me tighter. "I'd never, ever think that of you. You're one of these rare people who'd hit the ground running wherever you'd go. You don't need me. You don't need anyone. Staying away from you was my small contribution to make it public knowledge, to protect you."

The new information wipes out entirely the self-doubt I've harbored when my affection wasn't reciprocated, the scenarios I conjured combined with Jen's past. It takes a toll on me, implementing the new information along with the intensity of the sex and the emotions it's flooded to the surface.

I'm exhausted down to my bones. So, Hudson, true to his promise, keeps me safe. He kisses my lips in a gentleness that reaches to the depths of my soul, tightening his embrace on me. I sigh, nestling both hands on his taut chest, curling my knees up until I'm in a little, sheltered cocoon.

"Look at me," he whispers, and I do. Through heavy-lidded eyes, in the darkness, I see him.

"I said I'm falling for you, but I lied. I love you, Avery. I feel it everywhere. I love you, your smart mouth, your soulful eyes, your sense of humor, your tender heart." He nuzzles my nose, spreading heat, care, and belonging with an equal intensity as his words did. "I just love you. I realized it late, too late, and I'll do whatever you ask me to make up for the years wasted."

No words materialize, none. I love him too, of course, I do, but when I try to say it through the sensory overload plaguing me, my mouth gapes by a fragment. Nothing more.

"Little one." He pulls the blanket over my shoulders, gently moving my head to the crook of his neck where I'm comforted by the traces of his aftershave and sweat, and us. "You don't have to say it back. You're here, you came for me. That's all that matters."

Little Blue

"Thank you," I peep out as my eyelids close in on me.

In repetitive, monotonous motions, Hudson caresses my hair, murmuring into my ear, "That's it, go to sleep."

I want to thank him again. I want to live inside his shirt. I want to scream just how much I love him.

But before I get to do any of that, my body succumbs to Hudson's.

And I fall asleep.

CHAPTER SIXTEEN
Hudson

I can't recall the last time I enjoyed a Sunday morning, kicking back in my breakfast room with a view of my garden wearing a smile as I sip my coffee.

During the two years before Lucy, my ex-wife, had confessed to me her issues with our marriage, of her consequent infidelity, weekends were nonexistent for me.

Hours upon hours of my time were devoted to studying trends in the beverage markets, planning strategic moves to drive profits to our company and thus our shareholders, working relentlessly to prove that hiring a thirty-one-year-old CFO with no prior experience in this particular position was the right choice.

Our marriage and she weren't my priority by then and our love simmered to nothing, but it still hurt like a motherfucker hearing how for over a year she'd preferred giving her heart to another man behind my back instead of talking it out, or asking for a divorce, which I would've given had she only asked.

And though it messed with my ability to trust, my capacity to love was left intact. I'm reminded of it whenever I look at Avery.

Or whenever I hear her nearing.

Small footsteps pad down the stairs, then the living room's floor, announcing my love's arrival before her effervescent figure appears in the entryway between the two rooms. Her legs are bare, her white shorts unaccounted for. She didn't bother wearing a bra either, I notice when she prances up to me, giving me a chaste kiss with a mouth smelling of my minty toothpaste.

"Morning, Sir." A sneaky grin creeps up her cheeks, still puffy due to long hours of sleep.

"Morning, little blue." Her teasing gets me rock hard in an instant, but intrigue locks me in place. More than I ache to drag her over to ride me on that chair, I'm hooked on watching her mysterious plan unfold.

I spin my chair to the wide pathway connecting the room I'm at to the kitchen, zeroing in on Avery who makes herself at home.

"Breakfast?" Avery's blue eyes glint as she glimpses me over her shoulder.

Little Blue

"I'd appreciate it." I indulge her, even when food is at the bottom of my list of needs.

My tongue sweeps across my bottom lip, my arms folding over my chest. Her smile widens at my gratitude, the genuine joy beaming across her face reminds me of our days at the office, where every praise I gave her rewarded me with similar exuberance.

"Coming right up." She twirls back, her long hair bouncing down her slender shoulders. The fluorescent lights from the fridge illuminate her when she opens the stainless-steel door, browsing the shelves. "What do we have here?"

Out of the entirety of my fully stored fridge, Avery decides the bottom drawers will contain the products she'll use for our meal.

"Vegetables work?" she asks, her voice muffled through the blood pounding in my ears.

The rush of blood is caused by the peeking of her round ass from beneath her boy shorts, by the primal need to put her over my lap and spank her red, see how much she can take today when she's still raw.

Yet all of it's concealed behind a mask of steel. "Go ahead."

"Eggs?" Avery twists for my approval, this time powerless to hold her eyes to mine. Her gaze drops to my shirtless chest, and from there pivots to the noticeable bulge in my sweatpants.

I don't concern myself with fixing it, if it means she'll continue looking at me like food matters little to her, too.

"Please."

"How do you like them..." She swallows, her fingers wrenching the hem of her shirt. "...Sir?"

Sweet and yet so fucking seductive, Avery stares at me, pleading for an answer on what she can do to please me.

"Scrambled," I respond with the first thing that pops to my mind, then add, "Three eggs, don't burn them."

Determination paints her face swiftly before she returns to retrieve the ingredients for the breakfast I doubt either of us will eat. I'm hanging on a thread as is, and I'm betting she is too.

And this treading on the edge of a cliff, it yanks me out of my role altogether. "How wet is your cunt, Avery?"

The steel spatula she's holding clashes in a clamor on the gray countertop. Her head bows low, her shoulders rise to her ears, then fall.

There's no need to reiterate the question since I'm pretty fucking confident my fingers would come soaked out of her pussy, one I'd much rather eat for the first meal of the day than whatever's in my fridge.

Little Blue

"I'm not hearing an answer." I raise my voice an octave higher. "Not seeing my breakfast being prepared, either."

Avery grips the spatula, half-twisting her head. Her cheeks are on fire, her eyes burning.

"Really wet," she whispers.

"Is that so?"

"Yes." She doesn't give me a chance to toy with her further by admonishing her on the lack of Sir, sifting through the cupboards above her. "Where do you keep the pans?"

My limits are torn seeing her ass peeking for the second time today, and I push up from my chair, eager to put my hands on her. Avery yelps when I wrap an arm around her torso to drag her to me, moaning when I bend her at the waist and lick the shell of her ear. Our connection is natural, with her back molding into my stomach, and how my cock fits between her butt cheeks.

How my heart forgets momentarily every filthy thing I wanted to do to her as soon as she gives me her profile, saying, "I just love being hugged by you, Sir."

I slip my hand into her panties, telling her wordlessly that there'll be no cooking today. She moans, her ass pressing to me, her parted lips seeking mine while the heel of my palm pushes to her clit, my index and middle finger curling into her pussy.

Ever Marks

Which, like she described, is really, very fucking wet.

"Love hugging you, too. Always wanted to." I kiss her temple, inhaling her scent. "I dreamt of holding you, refused to settle for anything less for three years, ever since I laid my eyes on the most precious,"—she gasps from the forceful way I pull on her nipple with my other hand, of my teeth sinking into her bare shoulder—"sweetest, hottest…"

"Hudson." My name echoes in equal measures of pain and pleasure.

"…who's also the funniest, brightest, and most beautiful woman I've ever met."

It's then, when the waterfall of images of our office days pours in front of my eyes, that an idea permeates my head. I twist her, gripping her from beneath her knees to heft her up. Her ankles link around me, hands clasping behind my neck, blue, sparkling eyes entwining with mine.

"What about breakfast?"

I carry her to the stairs, smirking. "We'll have to reschedule. You and I, we're getting out of here."

Avery pushes closer to me, her fingers digging into the back of my head. "Out where?"

"To the office," I grunt, crushing her to one of the walls in the hallway, sucking on her neck. "I'm about to show you at exactly which point I saw you, where I fantasized of owning your teasing, little ass."

"Wait."

"What is it?" I stop whatever it is I'm doing, looking at her through narrowed eyes.

"I…" Her smooth, delicate palms cup my stubbled jaw, pulling me to her until our foreheads press together. "I love you. I wanted to tell you before you fucked my brains out and left my brain a big puddle of mush. Which, by the way, is why I couldn't reciprocate yesterday. So, I'm saying it now. I love you, Hudson. I love you so much."

I'm not a sentimental guy. Didn't shed a tear when my ex told me she was having an affair, never in my life felt so emotional I couldn't speak. But as I discovered the past week, with Avery I am not myself.

I'm hers.

A fierce pang slices my heart in two, the realization she's actually here saying it mending it back into one, whole piece.

"Hudson?"

Her voice, the only one I wish would repeat my name for as long as I live, revives me. "I'm here. I'll always be, blue. I love you."

Ever Marks

I drown our breaths, hearts, thoughts in a final all-consuming kiss before completing the journey upstairs and out of the house.

CHAPTER SEVENTEEN

Avery

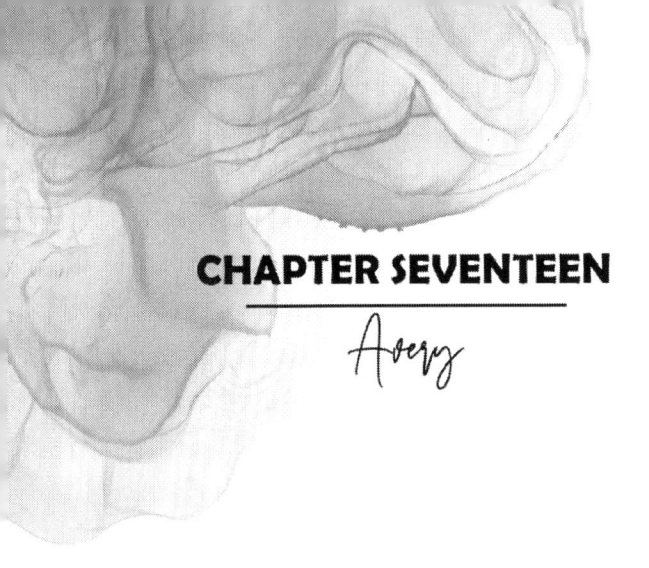

"I'm not so sure about this anymore." I sneak a glance behind my shoulder at the dark halls of my old workplace.

Hudson sits in front of me behind his desk in one of his expensive midnight-blue suits, a white dress shirt, and a tie a shade darker than the suit. He shaved earlier, then styled his hair so there's no strand out of place. A man ready to embark on a regular workday, just like any other.

I, on the other hand, am overwhelmingly underdressed, wearing a lilac mini-Jersey dress and my white chucks, free of any sort of underwear on Hudson's demand. See, when Hudson told me to bring a change of clothes in his gruff, sexy tone, this scenario, or any notion of us leaving his home, wasn't what I had in mind.

Ever Marks

But even if I had my office clothes on, it would hold little to no importance should someone enter the building and catch us in the vulnerable position we were about to put ourselves in and I'm petrified.

The last time I was here, the day I said goodbye to these offices in favor of Pearl Wilde, I departed with my shoulders straight and chin up high, respected.

And Hudson, he sacrificed his marriage to get where he is.

Apprehension lodges in my heart, anxiety leaps at my throat. I shift from my right foot to the left one within a safe distance from a man I admitted to loving less than an hour ago.

Hudson sees it.

"Little blue." Using *the* tone.

My attention whips back to him, to the present moment. My gaze focuses on him and not on the million anxiety-filling scenarios running amok in my mind. He pushes the button to shut down the smart blinds, blocking the inside of the office, his green eyes fixated on mine.

"Come here." His authoritative tone, along with the newfound privacy, compels me to him. I drift closer, hesitating at the edge of his desk.

He lowers his head, gazing up at me. "You're safe. After the public announcement of Brandy as our newest celebrity endorser, the majority of the company is out on

Little Blue

summer vacation. My department finished the quarterly reports. I wouldn't compromise your integrity, what you've worked for, not ever."

The last claws the trepidation had on my heart wither and die. I'm secure with him, here and everywhere. And I'm ready for him. I strut seductively toward Hudson who's patting his thigh.

"That's right. Over here."

When I'm within arms' reach, Hudson grabs my hand, spins me so my ass is to him, hikes my dress up then holds my lower belly, pinning me to him.

His impressive cock pokes my behind, his hand curling around my neck from the front of my body only serves to heighten the sparks of electricity his proximity sends to my brain.

Another flare of arousal fires me up as Hudson's teeth scrape my ear, sucking my earlobe. "I've been so hard for you in this office for years, spent the days admiring you and nights jerking off to thoughts of you."

"Show me." I swallow, gulping against the flexing of his fingers. "Please."

"I have every intention to." He angles his fingers to my pussy that's already aching with burning, uncontainable desire.

Knowing this eligible man who could have any woman of his choice was celibate for me is enough of a turn on without the mental picture of him in the shower, his cock in his fist, hand braced on the shower tiles, water dripping down his muscled back, every slow and fast stroke meant for me.

Fuck.

His hand leaves my throat, arranging some papers on his desk. He doesn't let me wonder for long, explaining, "Rina dropped off the analysis of the company's monthly sales at the beginning of the week. Remember this one?"

"M-hmm." They used to be my responsibility, like anything that involved handling Hudson. I envied her for assuming this part of my job, for working this close to him.

"I'm not showing it to you to make you jealous," he says, reading my mind. "Not like you need any reason to, but just so you know my meetings with her are contained to the bare minimum, strictly business. I. Want. No one. Except. You."

To prove his point, Hudson finds my lips, sliding his tongue on mine. "Even before you were mine," he breathes. "I was yours. That hasn't changed because you were gone. Understand?"

The sincerity in his eyes is overwhelming, a force. I'm thankful to be held by him, otherwise, my feeble limbs would've failed me. "Yes, Sir."

Little Blue

He studies me carefully, observing whether I'm telling him the truth. Once satisfied, we're back at the papers.

"Hands on the desk," he commands, maneuvering me to my feet while sliding an arm over my thighs to brace me.

I do as I'm told. Hudson flips the skirt of my dress up, kicks my legs a tad wider, his rough and loving touch putting pressure on my back to lift my ass so my cunt is open for him. The chill of the AC on my arousal shocks my senses, a second before Hudson assumes complete control of them by flicking his tongue from my clit up.

My forearms collapse to the cold desk, while Hudson's grip tightens.

"So, I've had my hands full this week. All the way through the weekend." Every syllable makes my pussy infinitely more sensitized, having Hudson speaking directly to my hole, licking me at the end of the sentence. "Would you be a good girl for me, tell me if there's something important that should come to my attention?"

None of the numbers add up, a whirlpool of black and white and splashes of the yellow marker. And though I'm yearning to please him, dying to be his good girl, I'm so deep into the maze of desire he's erected I wouldn't be able to read my proper name if it was written in huge caps in bold, black Sharpie across the entire wall.

"I…I can't." Desperation seeps into my surrender, tears pricking my eyes.

A loud smack brands my bare ass. The sudden pain throws me into the here and now, accompanied by Hudson's instructions. "I heard that one before, and you still pulled through."

"I…"

Slap.

I pull my lips in, shutting my eyes to contain the searing sensation. The sting of pain makes way for the tingles of pleasure, which is when Hudson decides to strike me again, three consecutive times. On the same exact spot.

"Try now." He traces his lips on the wounded flesh, unhurried open-mouthed kisses ending in my center. The soft sensation is traded with his open palm, pressed strong enough to remind me of the earlier hurt it inflicted. "Don't you want to please me?"

"I do." For fuck's sake, every bit of me does. "But…"

Slap. Slap.

"No buts. Well, except for this one." His harsh grabbing of what must be my red ass sends me to the space no one before Hudson carried me to. The man I'm failing by staying silent, by admitting defeat.

I blink, trying to clear my mind at least partially so I can think.

Little Blue

I can do this. "Lodus Beer sales are up this m—month." My speech falters when he rewards me in the form of two fingers stroking my pussy. "Probably because it's summer. Fuck. And the festival you sponsored."

He dips them inside, dragging his fingertips on my walls. "Very good. I'm so impressed that you remembered."

His praise is a tender embrace, in complete contrast to the deep thrust of a third finger into me. I clench around him, drowning and floating and everything in the between. "Thank you, Sir."

"Come on my face, Avery." He replaces his fingers with his tongue, fucking my pussy relentlessly while punching and kneading my clit. "Come on me, now."

My body shudders, fingers clinging to the flat wooden surface of his desk, nails scratching it. It's going to leave a mark, but I don't care. I'm powerless where my physical reactions are concerned, brazenly riding Hudson's mouth.

"Look at me." He separates from me after dragging out my orgasm for as long as he could. I oblige, colliding with dark green eyes, a predatory gaze.

One of his arms still holds me upright, while the other swipes a travel-size bottle out of the inside of his jacket, popping the lid open. I know where it's going. I know I want it.

Ever Marks

I want Hudson every-fucking-where.

I'll work for it, too, which, by the smirk rising on his lips, is exactly what he has planned for me. Whatever it takes to have him all over me.

I'll do it.

CHAPTER EIGHTEEN
Hudson

"Now, what would you have us do to keep the momentum for the winter?"

Avery's mouth twitches, satiated from her last orgasm, yet fully prepared for my question before I asked her.

"Lean toward what we did to our tequila line last year when Ragsdill started a price war against us."

My girl's eagerness to satisfy me blows my mind. There's no way I'm going to stop her. My erection thickens, seeing how even with my lube-coated thumb caressing her ass and more heat blossoming in her, she finds the wherewithal to complete her task.

I missed this. I missed working with her, bouncing ideas back and forth, even when it regards marketing and not finance. I missed getting so rock-hard off her wicked brain.

The scent of her arousal, her pink little pussy in my face, and her ass ready to be fucked are a precious bonus.

So, I play my part. "What will we sell as a beer bundle? For the winter?"

"Do you honestly think I'm that boring, to offer you more of the same?" Her breathless voice shoves the pestering notions of going back to work without her to the dark place where they belong. We'll make it work.

"Hold on to the table." I grab both sides of her ass, pulling her to me, stretching her arms. Her thighs clench when I move the hand that's wrapping her legs to the glistening hole, sliding it to her clit and patting her lightly, then stroking her. "Tell me, then."

Her head drops and I marvel at her barely-contained moans.

"*I can't* isn't an answer I'm willing to accept, little one."

"Another taste." Her hand slaps on the desk, hard. "Ginger or I don't know, let fucking Rina come up with something for once." Avery inches her butt closer, pleading to have more of me, waiting for her reward which she so clearly deserves.

Little Blue

"Christ, you tell me one time *I love you* and I forget what a greedy slut you are." Without a preamble, I remove my fingers from her delicious clit to spank her.

"Yes."

"Yes, what?" I guide her forward to allow me to get up to standing, shoving the chair behind me.

"Yes, Sir."

The slightest nudge of my thumb, the tiniest circles, widen her hole. "Look at you, ready to take my cock in your ass."

Her head, hidden by the curtains of light brown locks, bobs once. I'm aware speaking takes a toll on her when my thumb is deep inside her, but I don't ease up. I grip her hair in my hand, exposing her flushed face to me. "Do. You. Want. It?"

"Y-yeah."

I tug hard. The veins in her delicate neck pump with blood, as does my cock. "Words, little."

"Sir." As soon as I hear the strength returning to her, I unbuckle my belt. "Fuck my ass, please. I need you to fuck me there." A low hum echoes from those plump lips of her at the sound of my zipper being pulled down. "I need to be filled with you."

"There you go." I retrieve the small bottle from my jacket, lubing my cock. Before I toss it to the floor, I squeeze it over her ass, rubbing it into her crack. Even though she wants it, couldn't be more ready for it, I'm not risking having it hurt her. "I'll start slow, but be sure I'm shoving every inch of my dick up your greedy ass."

"Oh, God."

"No, baby." Parting her legs even wider, I guide myself to her back entrance. "Much better than him."

Despite the tension in her face from the hold I have on her, her hole is lax as I slide the head in. "You like that?"

"Love it," she gasps. "Fuck me. Use me. Please."

And I do, sliding farther into her, wrapping more of myself with her addictive heat. I'm halfway in, halting as I wonder if my Avery will tolerate however rough I give it to her. She turns her beautiful eyes to me, mouthing again *Please*.

Just the answer I needed. I plunge into her, the base of my cock slapping her ass.

"Hudson, fuck." Her expression is that of uncontained ecstasy. She's raw. Beyond desperation.

"Think I liked God better," I smirk, picking up the pace of my thrusts. "But Hudson works, too."

The short laugh she breathes transforms into a guttural moan the harsher my pummels are. We take full advantage of the empty offices, cursing, groaning, almost drowning out the noises our sweaty bodies make as they smack together.

Little Blue

Her orgasm ripples through her, clenching and unclenching around me, and I experience it with an unimaginable force. It surges from her to my soul, my balls tightening a second before I come deep inside my lover, where I belong.

I drape my body on top of hers, careful when I remove myself out of Avery.

"I love you, my beautiful, good girl." My lips, hungry for her skin, kiss the curve of her spine, her shoulder blades, her damp nape. "Nothing makes me happier than you do. Only you."

She twists, flashing her teeth in a snarky smile. "What about Rina?"

"That mouth." We both laugh as I spank her ass, nibbling on her ear. I pick her up gently, placing her on my chair and pulling on my boxers and pants. "I love it."

"I love you, too." Her wide eyes fixate on me when I don't sit down. "Where are you going?"

"To the restroom then the kitchen to get you a warm cloth and tea." I kiss her damp forehead, brushing my fingers in her hair and over her jaw. "Then I'll take you home."

She brightens, a spectacular illumination exceeding nature's most brilliant of sunrises. I feel love, true love, pulling at the strings of my heart for the very first time, and I'd do anything in my power to protect it.

Ever Marks

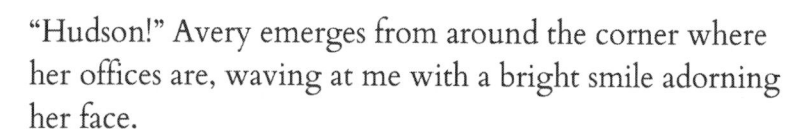

"Hudson!" Avery emerges from around the corner where her offices are, waving at me with a bright smile adorning her face.

She's wearing the outfit I dictated to her before we left her apartment this morning—cream-colored high heel sandals, a white, ankle-length accordion skirt, and a pale-blue blouse to match the color of her eyes, and her hair in the ponytail I've tormented more than once this last week.

My lips tug up at my little one, an impulsive reflex whenever she's around. We've been testing the waters of our relationship in the privacy of either her apartment or mine, but there's no denying that what we have far outweighs any casual infatuation. Three years were plenty of wait, and neither of us needs further proof of how right we are for each other.

So, this Friday, we set out to have a lunch date. Making us an official couple.

"Avery." I cup her cheek, angling her head toward me for a chaste kiss. Her scent carries to me, as fresh and sweet as it was a few hours ago. "I missed you."

Little Blue

"Missed you, too." Her blue eyes reflect the sun, a sight I'm pained to depart when I guide her into the restaurant.

I rest my hand on the small of her back, using the other one to pull on the barn door handle for Avery to enter.

"Mr. Kent." The hostess recognizes me from the many business lunches I've held here locating my reservation, smiling politely.

Barely acknowledging her, I gaze down at the vibrant woman by my side. It might be early for Avery to hear it, so I withhold my thoughts to myself, but I'm itching to correct the hostess by telling her soon-to-be Mr. *and* Mrs. Kent.

Hey, when you know, you know.

"I can't stop missing you," I whisper close to her ear, an intimate gesture rather than a necessity since it's obvious no one would hear us over the hustle of the open kitchen, the conversations of the restaurant's patrons, or the jazz music.

We're led through the spacious tasting menu restaurant to the back, where I reserved our spot. Besides the food, I crave eating up Avery's stories of her childhood, college years, work. Hell, even her love for biking and the unique places she stumbles upon on her rides.

Ever Marks

She's fascinating. Her joy of life—a side of her she maintained hidden to uphold her professional persona—keeps me up until the small hours of the night.

"All I see whenever I look at my desk," I continue, "is your ass held up high, and my cock ramming into it."

"Here's your table," the hostess says just as Avery gasps. "Something wrong? We're packed, but if it's not suitable, I'm sure we can make accommodations for Mr. Kent."

"Up to you." I rub slow circles on Avery's back, my tone verging on playful.

Avery glances up at me, shaking her head slightly. "No, no. This is perfect."

"*You're* perfect," I murmur, squeezing her to me one final time.

I pull out the chair facing the kitchen for Avery to enjoy their show, then sit, listening to our hostess's explanation of today's menu and the seasonal flavors incorporated in it. She could've told us they serve raw lemons for all I care.

With Avery, every place, every day, every second, is equal to a vacation on a tropical island. Whatever I smell, hear, see or eat, is paradise.

"That's unfortunate you said that," Avery coaxes me from my daydreams.

"Oh?"

Little Blue

She talks in her husky bedroom voice when she leans forward, "Because we're in this nice place and the food smells amazing, and I won't be able to enjoy it when I'm so fucking wet."

"Who says I can't take care of both?" From beneath the table, I shove my foot between hers, kicking her legs apart. I outstretch my arm, caressing her soft cheek, and am about to tell her how it'd please me to feed her while she imagines me going down on her under the table.

But a familiar voice stops me from saying that.

"Hudson? Avery?" Albert Benjamin, the COO of Whitlock hovers over our table.

Matter of fact, he stops me from saying anything at all.

CHAPTER NINETEEN
Avery

"Are you two...?" Albert waves a finger from Hudson to me. Pauses. Then lets out a low whistle, his mouth splits in two, he smiles so wide. "You two dating? Avery, who would've guessed you've got daddy issues?"

The Chief of Operations, a short, older man, didn't consider tact a necessity when handling people like the rest of the population, a characteristic which never bothered me until this day. I'm speechless—because really, how does one reply to such a blunt, assuming, remark—so, he diverts his attention to Hudson, casting his small, entertained, brown eyes toward him.

My boyfriend.

My Sir.

Ever Marks

The one who's supposed to protect me, sits there silent, his hand withdrawn from my cheek, the side of his shoe no longer lying against my ankle. And it's this silence that speaks volumes. It latches on my skin, slides inside my body through my pores, poisons my bloodstream, crawls, and sinks its claws into my insecurities.

He's ashamed of being seen with me, of the name-calling.

From here, the road for him to break our relationship off isn't far, and I sure as shit am not planning to wait for him to carry out the heartbreaking sentence for me.

"Avery doesn't—" Hudson starts.

I'm already scrambling to my feet, pushing the chair back. "Sorry, Hudson, Albert. My team just texted, our CEO asked for me. I have to go. Goodbye."

I turn to Hudson, emphasizing the word with hopes he'd understand I don't want another day or two of grace where he'll sell me emotions he isn't ready to stand behind.

My heels click on the wooden floor, my steps hurried to avoid the dam of tears from opening in the middle of the populated restaurant. A thousand thoughts attack my consciousness as I rush forward, blurring my vision. I'm incapable of deciphering them since my heart races a mile a minute, and not caring to understand. I have to get away, that's all.

Little Blue

"Avery!" I hear him behind me, trying to manipulate me with the voice I adhere to every single time.

For a second, I do it again. My quick steps falter from the yearning to be held by him. I love Hudson. I adore him, I'm connected to him. I need him. Which is exactly why leaving for good is crucial. When I give my heart like that, I expect to receive everything in return.

And I break into a sprint.

"Avery," he calls me again.

I don't listen, excusing myself for weaving past customers who opened the door to walk inside. The summer's sun is blinding, not like it would stop me either. I pick up the pace, running faster when I take the corner toward my office.

People going to and from their lunch breaks clear the path for me, turning their heads without saying a word to the woman who cry-runs in the streets on this fine noon on a Friday. I ignore them, ignore the red light for the crosswalk.

But I can't ignore the long, ear-piercing honk of the blue sedan coming at me.

Strong fingers curl around my bicep, hurling me into the taut lean body it's attached to.

"Avery, weren't you looking?" He grips both my arms, drawing my chest to his. His gaze wanders over my face, my neck, my arms, a mental checklist of uninjured body parts. Thanks to him, I'm in one piece. At the sight of my unharmed body, Hudson envelopes me in a bone-crushing hug, pressing his chin to the top of my head.

"Don't ever do that. Don't ever endanger yourself, I wouldn't survive without you."

I pinch my eyes shut to bid the tears to stop. They slow down, enough for me to speak without sounding pathetic. "You didn't even acknowledge me there. You didn't put him in place, didn't own up to our relationship." Placing my fists between us, I shove him from me, staring into his eyes. "Did you have us sitting in the dark corner in the back so no one would see?"

"What?" He holds me at an arms' length, his eyes level with mine to make sure I hear what he says. "No. No, no, no, you're not even close."

"Then what is it?" I wipe the mascara that undoubtedly smeared down my cheeks. "If you were confident about this, us, if this is what you want, you'd have shut him right up. Plain and simple. Yet you didn't. Explain to me why you didn't say anything. I'm lost, Hudson." I sob. "It hurts."

"Blue." He maintains a safe distance. "First, I took us to sit in the back because I love having you to myself, to listen to you, to catch every word you say uninterrupted. I wanted to touch you less than socially acceptable since

Little Blue

we're going out with your friends tonight and like I said, I'm aching to have my hands on you, always."

The words he says resonate with me, regardless of how they're still lacking.

"The way I imagined introducing our relationship to our coworkers wasn't like this." Swiping tears from my cheeks, he inches closer, his warm caress loosening the knot in my stomach. "Like you're a dirty secret they happened to stumble upon. I planned to take you to the End of the Summer corporate event, so no one would doubt my devotion and love to you."

His chest expands, his forehead pressing to mine. I don't dare resist him.

"When Albert showed up, I was afraid of what he'd make of you, not me. Then he proved me right, and I had to bite my tongue real fucking hard so I wouldn't regret my response, or worse, punch him in the face for ever disrespecting you. Fuck, if it wouldn't have landed me jail time where I'd be far from you, I probably would have. Screw Whitlock, screw everyone."

I see him, his intentions, his honesty. And I start crying for a whole other reason. "I'm sorry. I'm so sorry I ran away."

"Avery. Little blue." Hudson encapsulates my cheeks in his potent hands, drawing me to his lips. His touch, as they flutter across my face, soothes me. I don't need him to be harsh right now, and he knows it. He knows me. "I love you. I want you. Fucking starving for you, because of how long we've waited. There's absolutely not one person in this universe I'd like to share my life with other than you."

He shakes his head, casting his gaze downward. "Fuck, I meant to postpone it. I can't anymore." He bites his bottom lip, and then I watch him lower to one knee with new, unshed tears brimming in my eyes. "Avery Myers, will you do me the utmost honor and be my wife?"

It's crazy. It's too fast. It's irrational.

But it's Hudson. My Hudson.

He'll be my rock, my shelter, the most wonderful partner, and surely the best father to our future children when the time comes.

It's a no-brainer.

"Yes." My ponytail bobs frantically. "Yes, I'll marry you."

He's on his feet in a heartbeat, crushing his lips to mine, kissing me as bystanders clap and cheer for us.

"I love you, little blue."

"I love you, too."

EPILOGUE

Hudson

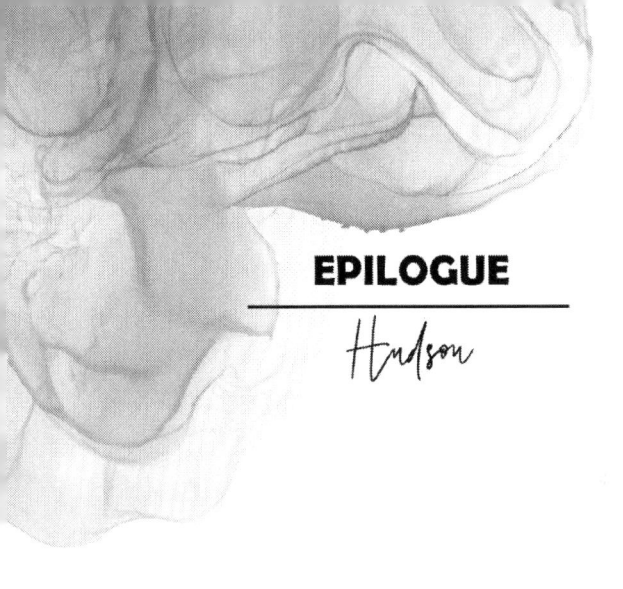

"Little one." My tone is harsh, a contrast to the warmth swiping over me.

"Da-da." Rosalee, our one-year-old is wide awake in her crib at what should be her nap time.

"Yes, I am Da-da alright." I rise from my workstation to the corner her mother and I have allocated for our firstborn.

We set an identical one in her room, our bedroom, and the living room since we tend to work from our laptops all around the house. Having our baby comfortable with us has become our number one priority.

I gaze down at my daughter, at the charming smile and light brown hair she inherited from her mother, and the blue and green eyes she got from the both of us. She's

Ever Marks

exquisite, a perfect mashup of me and the other love of my life.

When I pick her up, she nestles right into my chest, chuckling and gripping my T-shirt, the same routine she knows to expect from the man who'll always be there for her.

"I thought I heard my rascal over here." Avery comes in from the kitchen, grinning from ear to ear.

She's been prepping our Sunday lunch. Splashes of tomato sauce stain her turquoise shirt and white shorts, a spot coloring her left cheek. It means I'll have to choose another outfit for her, but I don't mind.

Because it means I'll get to take what she's wearing off.

"Ma-ma!"

That is, whenever sweet Rosalee decides sleeping is in order.

My wife closes the distance between us, amused by her daughter's exuberance. "The Bolognese is on the stove so I'm free. Want to hand her over to me, get another couple of hours on *Cotton for All*?"

Soon after our engagement, Avery and I agreed on the importance of nurturing our relationship first and foremost. Both of us quit our old jobs, opting to start our own business of consulting for retail companies so we can work flexible hours and be able to do at least a large part of it at home.

We're a team, the best partners who complete each other. It shows in the results we bring in—Avery working her magic in the marketing aspect, while I contribute from knowledge in finance and strategic planning—as it does in the flourishing of our relationship between ourselves and our daughter.

I kiss the top of Avery's head, inhaling the scents of Italian cooking. Of her. "I need to wrap something up here, but after that, I'm yours." I tickle Rosalee's soft belly with my left hand, my ring glinting under the late morning sunlight streaming from the window. "And yours."

"And we are yours. Always."

She stretches out her arms for me to hand Rosalee over to her, excited as ever to embrace our best creation. Before I do, I study the wonderful woman by my side, wondering how I ever got so lucky.

"Come here," I command her in my stern voice, the one I know gives her a sense of belonging, of being protected and cherished.

Avery's arms drop to her side and she comes to me. She's careful not to say Sir in front of Ros, and yet I can feel the name pouring from my little in her eyes, her shy smile, the anticipation brimming within her for me to kiss her lips.

She's been such a good girl, though, that I don't let her wait that long.

"I love you," I say to both of them when I shift our daughter to her mom. "Daddy will be with you soon."

"Can't wait." Avery blushes, telling me before she turns to leave, "And love you, too."

The End.

About the Author
Writing edgy spicy novellas, addicted to HEAs, and an avid plant lady.

Stay in Touch!

Newsletter for new releases: https://bit.ly/3c3K2nt

Instagram: https://bit.ly/3QQ3Nh4

TikTok: https://www.tiktok.com/@evamarkswrites

Facebook Group: https://bit.ly/3LnFpln

Website: https://www.evamarkswrites.com/

My books: https://amzn.to/3pnp5XE

Coming October 31, 2022

Little Halloween

This holiday he plans on a special trick and treat for her…

After overcoming our differences, I'm finally engaged to Hudson, my old boss and millionaire CFO.

We're madly in love and I can't complain when he constantly cherishes, coddles me and says I'm his good girl. I can't and won't, even if I miss his harsh domineering side at times.

But my fiancé, who reads me like a book, can tell I have doubts, and he knows just how to put them to rest.

This Halloween, at an adult club party, Hudson will show me and everyone around once and for all exactly what my Sir is made of.

TW: Bondage, BDSM, pet play, sex club, exhibitionism, a bit of degradation and a whole lot of love.

Available for pre-order.

Coming December 2022
Toy Shop

Time to strap on, because class is about to start...

Working in an adult toy shop doesn't make me an expert on the matter. Quite the opposite, actually. My experience with my last boyfriend all but destroyed my interest in it. Until billionaire Alistair Cromwell bulldozed his way into my life.

He's unlike anyone I've ever known—dominant, harsh, but oddly tender. And he's more than willing to educate me on every product in the shop.

In fact, he insists on it.

He tells me I'm his good girl. That only I can save him from his demons. I want that desperately. But I also want the one thing he doesn't think he can ever give me.

His heart.

Well, he's about to learn that while I'm not worldly when it comes to sex, I do know a thing or two about love. And I'm going to teach him every bit as much as he's taught me...

TW: Bondage, BDSM, edge play, breath play, sex toys, a bit of degradation, death of a relative, past trauma.

Available for pre-order.

Made in the USA
Columbia, SC
12 October 2022